Praise for *Courage to Love*

Courage to Love is a well-written, fast-paced story outlining cultural and religious differences. It involves several different characters and is written in a *Da Vinci Code* like style from chapter to chapter. The attention and respect paid to all sides of the fight—the religion, customs and language—makes for a compelling insiders look into the Israeli-Palestinian conflict. There is no bias for one religion, province, or people over another; but more of a story of how even in the most extreme cases of hatred, peace and love can be found. It's a very visual story that lends itself to multimedia—the printed page, film, and T.V.—as its ripe content makes it a story of interest to everyone.

K. Cannary, reviewer and editor.

Courage to Love is a valuable and powerful story...I hope it attracts a wide audience.

Warren J.R., Order Franciscan Minor.

In *Courage to Love*, the story's two main characters are programmed in the name of their opposite causes. What impresses me the most is that the power of love unites them. Through the two young teenagers, the older generation is transformed as well to opt for life over death and love over hate. What a powerful text for young readers worldwide.

Former president of a Middle Eastern university.

The main focus in all three major religions (Jewish, Christian & Muslim) is peace and love. Going back in time, we as humans have always ruined this notion with our greed and hate. Josh and Haja's story truly shows how love can triumph over all evils. The story is so fair to all sides, it is an inspiration.

Adib Nono, Orthodox Catholic and Islam scholar

I have been looking for a human scale story about the Middle East: but one that will both entertain and provoke. In short I believe *Courage to Love* is it. Not since Elie Wiesel has an author distilled these conflicts into such human terms. Put another way, while the story touches on significant issues, it is really a tale of two young people and their struggle to be allowed to love each other.

Bill Birrell, Filmmaker

courage to love

courage to love

a novel by **Robert Ellis**

TATE PUBLISHING *& Enterprises*

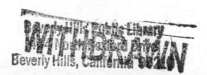

Published by Tate Publishing & Enterprises, LLC
127 E. Trade Center Terrace | Mustang, Oklahoma 73064 USA
1.888.361.9473 | www.tatepublishing.com

Tate Publishing is committed to excellence in the publishing industry. The company reflects the philosophy established by the founders, based on Psalm 68:11,
"The Lord gave the word and great was the company of those who published it."

Book design copyright © 2010 by Tate Publishing, LLC. All rights reserved.

Cover is a celebrated painting, Rosa Meditativa, by Salvador Dali, courtesy of 2008 Salvador Dali, Gala-Salvador Dali Foundation/Artists Rights Society (ARS) New York.
Cover design by Leah LeFlore
Interior design by Janae J. Glass

Published in the United States of America

ISBN: 978-1-60696-423-1
1. Fiction: Romance: Contemporary 2. Fiction: General
10.04.08

Throughout my life, my soul has seemed to record and mourn the numbers of soldiers and innocents who were killed in the wars of my time, from the Italian bombardment of Ethiopia and Spain in 1935-36, through the invasions of China, Czechoslovakia, WWII and the Holocaust, Hiroshima, Korea, Vietnam, the Middle East, Iraq and Afghanistan.

To stop this slaughter,
my soul extends to the world this desert rose.

—Robert Ellis

To all who dare to love

acknowledgements

Many thanks to my many friendly experts--in the fields of medicine, religion, chemistry, history, philosophy, film, and Middle Eastern history and politics—for their advice and encouragement in the preparation of this novel; and I respect their privacy: Arthur V., Barbara M., Bruce B. MD., Matthew B., Kim B., Bud A. MD., Daniel C., E E., George K., Shelly K., Jacob H., Yehuda H., James C. R., James R., Joshua C., John S., Richard S., Ju E., Li B., Lisa A., Lk E., Sean E., Marietta A.PHD, Mark C., Mohamad M., Margaret M,PHD., Rafe E., M.D., Steven B. MD., Susan S., Warren R., OFM, William D. T., Andrew W.

In an unusual growth process, editors of different backgrounds and ages also contributed clarity, accuracy and drama to these pages. My gratitude extends to early editor Patricia A. McLaughlin, Interim editor Sam Cruickshank of New Zealand, and Final Editors Kathleen Knapp and Raymond Gill; to Dr. Richard Tate, President, and the staff of Tate Publishing Enterprises, to cover design artist Leah Leflore and layout designer Janae Glass.

And I am deeply indebted to artist Salvador Dali.

All biblical references have been taken from the NKJV.

The song Aatini Nay (Hand Me the Flute) was penned by the Lebanese poet Khalil Gibran, and recorded by the international singer of Arabic songs, Fayrouz.

table of contents

prologue

"Two households, both alike in dignity,
In fair Mediterranea, where we lay our scene,
From ancient grudge break to new mutiny,
Where civil blood makes civil hands unclean.
From forth the loins of these two foes,
A pair of impetuous lovers risk their lives;
Whose misadventure'd piteous overthrows
Do, with their passion, bury their parents' strife.
The fearful passage of their terror-threatened love,
And the continuance of their parents' rage,
Which but their children's love naught could remove,
Is now the traffic of our novella's page,
The which, if you with patient heart attend,
What here shall miss, our toil shall strive to mend."

"Romeo and Juliet"
Opening Chorus, Scene 1, Act 1,
Written circa 1594-5. Amended,
with apologies to *William Shakespeare*

prologue in arabic

مقدمة

"عائلتان، في المقام متساويتان،

في حوض البحر المتوسط الرائق حيث نرسم مشهدنا،

العائلتان تدخلان في صراع جديد من بعد بغض قديم،

حيث أيديهم مدنسة بدماء بعضهم البعض.

من داخل هاتين العائلتين الغريمتين إلى النور يخرج،

عاشقان اثنان متهوران يغامران بحياتهما؛

وانقلاباتهما البائسة سيئة الطالع

تدفن، مع عشقهما، تخاصم آباءهما.

الطريق المخيف لحبهما المهدد بالذعر،

واستمرارية غضب آبائهما

الذي لا يمحوه سوى حب ابنيهما،

هو الآن وقود روايتنا،

والذي سيتابع تلك الأحداث بصبر،

ما لن تفهمه منها هنا، سنجاهد من أجل توضيحه."

الكورال الافتتاحي، المشهد 1، الفصل 1،

تم كتابتها حوالي 1594-5. مُعدلة، مع الاعتذار لـ /ويليام شيكسبير/

prologue in hebrew

פ ו ו ר ו ג

"שתי משפחות, דומות בהדרת כבודן,

בוורונה הנאווה, את סיפורן תפעלנה,

רענן למרי תפרוצנה קדומים ומטינת,

תגואלנה אזרח ידי אזרח בדם בו.

יגיחו האויבים אלה שני מחלצי,

נפשם שיחרפו, פזיזים אוהבים זוג;

ישליכו החמלה מעורר מזלם ביש,

תשוקתם בלהט אבות עימות ויקברו.

רודפיהם אימת חתת אהבתם נתיב,

כסנה בוער שעוד הוריהם וזעם,

בניהם אהבת מלבד ממאום יכבה שלא,

זה סיפורנו של אפו נשמת הם,

סיפור, שאם אליו תטו את לבבכם,

כל שתחמיצו נפעל בעמלנו לשקם."

"רומיאו ויוליה"

מעובד, בהתנצלות

בפני וויליאם שייקספיר

characters & locale

Courage to Love starts on March 18 and ends on April Fools Day, at a fictitious municipal hospital in Tel-Aviv-Yafo, Israel, "The Rose of Sharon."

The principals—among the hospital's patients, staff and outsiders, include:

Josh—Lt. Josh (Joshua) Isaacson, 21, an American patient injured while serving with the Israeli army. Born in Liberty Hill, South Carolina, USA., he withdrew from college after the 9/11/01 terrorist attacks on the United States, flew to Jerusalem, and, armed with his fluency in Hebrew and a strong belief that Mid-eastern peace would benefit his family, his country, and the world, joined the 'IDF,' the Israeli Defense Forces.

Ishmael—Ishmael bin Kanaan, 45, an Islamic imam, a scholar, and the secret leader of the hospital's jihad unit--an effort in worshipping Allah against nonbelievers and in defense of the Islamic faith. Born in Jericho, and growing up under the governments of Jordan, Israel, and the Palestine Authority, Ishmael was the youngest son of a large Palestinian farming family, and a goat shepherd in the hills. He played basketball as a schoolchild with local Hebrew and Christian boys, and the children of immigrants from Europe and the United States. During an IDF raid, Ishmael's father and their neighbor's daughter were killed; and, with a cash settlement granted by Israel, most of his family fled the country. Only Ishmael's elderly mother, Situ, and one daughter, Haja, remain with him.

Carol Ann—Carol Ann Tarcai, 41, born in Romania, is the warm-hearted fourth-floor nurse at the hospital. She and her father, a Holocaust victim, wandered from country to country before Ireland gave them temporary visas. The State of Israel granted them citizenship in 2000.

Noor—Noor-al-Nur, 27, a joyful staff nurse, is the assistant to the Chief of Surgery, and in training to become a doctor. Born in Amman, Jordan, she was named after Jordan's former American Queen Mother. Noor fled Jordan when her father forbade her to attend medical school with male students.

Haja—Hagar bin Kanaan, 17, Ishmael's daughter, is a Palestinian patient in the hospital, an angry-eyed teenager of arresting beauty, in active revolt against those responsible for her miserable life. Born on her family's peaceful orchard in Jericho, she was resettled in the over-crowded Jabaliya refugee camp in Gaza. Haja continues to be devoted to her remaining family, her father and elderly grandmother.

Doctor Ramzy—50, the hospital's Chief of Surgery and an Egyptian Coptic Christian. He starred in basketball at the University of South Carolina, before contracting a spinal disease in his pre-med years. His father, Dr. Ammon Ramzy, who was the hospital's Chief of Surgery in 1950, when the Jewish city of Tel Aviv merged with the Arab port of Jaffa, was born in Upper Egypt and traced his family's origins to the Ramses, Egypt's pharaohs from 2179 to1166 BC.

Rashid—Rashid Ibn Habas, 47, a Palestinian, manages Rose of Sharon's maintenance department. A college-trained mechanical engineer, he is the chief technician of the hospital's secret Jihad unit. Married, with four young daughters, he was born on the Jericho farm next to the bin Kanaan family's orchard; and his sister, Rashida, was killed in the IDF raid that killed Ishmael's father.

Daniel—Dr. Daniel Isaacson, 49 years old, is Josh's father and an Academic anesthetist at the Medical University of South Carolina. Dan was born in Vienna, the only child of a prominent East European Jewish banking family, and raised as an orthodox Jew. Nazi forces in World War II killed his father and most of the Isaacson family line.

Estee—Esther Isaacson, 43, Dr. Isaacson's wife and mother of their three children, Josh being the eldest. Estee is five months pregnant. She was born on a horse ranch near the mountain town of Liberty Hills, South Carolina, and was a nurse in training when she met Dr. Dan.

Doctor Levinson—Dr. Richard Levinson, 39, lanky and bushy-haired, is a native of Jerusalem. He is the director of the hospital's blood bank; received his medical training under Dr. Ramzy; and also holds a degree in Health Management from Ben Gurion University.

Al-Jabbar, 34, a hospital paramedic, third in command of the hospital's secret Jihad unit. He was born in Damascus, Syria, is married, with two children. An inconspicuous Israeli Arab with alert, observant eyes, he functions as Ishmael's eyes and ears.

Ariel—IDF Captain Ariel Cohen, 35, born in Haifa, is the hospital's Security Chief, charged with hospital safety. He had been wounded while on duty against Palestinian militants in Gaza. Married, with four children, he is a barrel-chested, steely-eyed, career soldier - always armed with stun gun, pistol, mace and knife.

Brother Byron, 67, a Franciscan friar born in Glasgow, Scotland, hospital out-patient under treatment for malignant skin cancer. Handsome and broad-shouldered with a shock of grey hair, he broke with the Episcopal Church 40 years ago, after his interracial marriage soured into a divorce. He now follows in the steps of St. Francis of Assisi, and holds a civil registrar's license from Lebanon.

General Ali Salmah, 49, a Palestinian born in Mecca, is a military commissioner for the West Bank. The general is a massive, medal-chested officer who carries out instructions from the Palestinian Authority, and coordinates combat actions with the state of Israel.

**Hebrew, Arabic, and other non-English words and phrases used in the text are written in italics the first time they are used. They are explained in the rear Glossary section of the book.

part one

chapter one

*Dawn, Thursday, March 18, 2004, Rose of Sharon Hospital's
basement outside the Operating Room...*

Josh is strapped to a surgical gurney while rocket-fired mortars
whine and explode nearby. Just above his head, one shell partially
buckles the ceiling. Cement rains onto his body and face. He
squeezes his blue eyes shut to help his mind escape. Instantly, he
is back crawling on hands and knees in yesterday's subterranean
Rafah tunnel, leading his Israel Defense Force patrol through the
three-foot wide, half-mile long wormhole fifty-seven feet beneath
the Egyptian-Gaza border. Streaks of crisscrossed high-clatter
fire sear the pitch-black. Shadowy Palestine arms smugglers fire
into his IDF squad... *I went ape like the frightened animals at both
ends of the tunnel and blazed away with my MAR 5.56. I counted
five bulls-eye probables until a rocket grenade ricocheted off the wall.
Then, some shrapnel tore into my abdomen. I woke up here.*

*Minutes earlier in the Mediterranean Sea's soupy fog cover-
ing Sharon's parking lot...*

    Imam Ishmael bin Kanaan lifted an electric wheelchair out of
his Toyota open-bed truck. He pointed with a long arm at the

shrouded mural of cactus red roses on the front wall of the five-story hospital. The imam's community *Mujahid* unit, active in the struggle for Islam, hidden among cypress and palm trees, took aim with AK-47s and 120 millimeter mortars at the main glass entranceway and upper windows and began firing.

Ishmael kept his reed-like body low against the damp sandy soil with all but his grey hunter's eyes hidden by his *kaffiyeh*, a black and white checkered headdress. He maneuvered the heavy, pearl-white chair toward the building's rear basement entrance. Inside, security guards completely confused by an attack that had never occurred before, scurried about amidst shredded cement, shattered glass and bleeding casualties, without knowledge of who was firing or why, mainly because Tel Aviv-Yafo's municipal hospital cared equally for all its four hundred thousand residents, including Israeli and Arab citizens, and was open to foreigners. Directions barking from all hospital loudspeakers ordered upper floor staff to move patients from glass window rooms into the safety of the hallways. Operating surgeons in the two basement amphitheater chambers closed open incisions on operations in progress and instructed nurses to keep the waiting scheduled patients strung out on gurneys along the circular basement corridor.

Reaching the rear entrance, Ishmael ran the chair up the ramp onto the deserted receiving dock and into the basement corridor. He steered right. With a passkey from his black pants, he unlocked the maintenance shop, dragged the chair inside, closed, and locked the door.

The forty-five-year-old Palestinian fighter/preacher

unrolled a small prayer carpet, dropped to his knees in the deserted workroom, bowed toward Mecca and intoned with piety, "*Allahu Akbar*." He touched his palms lightly on his handkerchief filled with red clay from Mecca, passed them over his aesthetic face in Islamic ritual. Rising into a crouch, withdrawing wrenches from his pockets, he prayed as he removed the left front wheel of the chair.

"I am here in the name of Allah the all-powerful, the all-knowing creator of the universe," he murmured in his native language, "I am here for Muslims who suffer under the Jewish and Christian invaders on our soil. I am here for my brothers who suffer humiliation under their occupation and want their holy land returned ... for Ali, my father and Rashida, family friend, murdered by the Israelis ...for Haja, my daughter, still in her youth, who will take vengeance in this wheelchair. I pray Allah, you turn her into an avenging angel of righteousness."

Ishmael felt his bloodline quivering inside him, back before the prophet Muhammad, back before his forefather Ibrahim, back to his Canaanite ancestors who cultivated the land. A shred of a folksong he had memorized as a boy in Jericho escaped his thin lips in a prophetic Arabic parody:

> "Joshua fought the battle of Jericho, Jericho, Jericho
> Joshua fought the battle of Jericho,
> And the walls came tumbling down ..."

The Mujahid leader rose to his feet and grasped the disabled chair with bone-hardened fingers trembling with rage. He dragged it among the pile of broken furniture in the shop. "Freedom. First step to freedom here." He straightened his checkered headscarf and vanished from the basement in purposeful strides.

～

Minutes later, outside Sharon's Operating Rooms in the basement corridor...

"Please, Nurse, my pain shot!" In panic and feeling abandoned, Josh whispered in Hebrew into the intercom clipped to his gurney. His body was in agony. The thick restraining straps kept him from turning his body. The loudspeaker's directions that alternated in Hebrew and Arabic echoed in the deserted hallway, "Keep away from the front entrance! Do not get close to windows. Code grey, code grey!"

"My shot, Nurse, now, please."

"Lieutenant Isaacson, the hospital is under attack."

"Morphine, a dozen Tylenols. Anything y'all have handy!" *Maybe my Southern drawl will do it.*

"Nurses cannot leave their stations. This is the switchboard operator." The intercom disconnected.

Josh struggled to open his IDL radiophone on his chest. He inched up the aerial and dialed a number. A murmur close by distracted him. Someone humming. "Nurse? Doctor? Who's there?"

The soft singing ceased.

"Hello?" His radiophone came alive. "Radio-Ops, I am under attack in a Tel Aviv hospital, can you reach my brother in USA? The number is 1-843-233-9901." He repeated the number several times, waiting an eternity. Finally, he heard a voice.

"Junior?" Smiling, he pumped up his voice. "What's going on, dude?"

"Josh!" Eighteen-year-old Daniel Isaacson, Jr., on the line in Charleston, South Carolina, instantly recognized his older brother's voice. "There's a lot of noise and I can hardly hear you. Where are you, Bro?"

"Stay with the baby back ribs and the Foster Freezes, Junior," Josh tried to keep bitterness out of his voice. "Don't try to change any hearts and minds ... I'm in Tel Aviv."

"What's going on?" Junior heard loud rumbling sounds.

"Junior, carry out our great desert reclamation plans. They're on my *Apple G4*. But work 'em in China or South America; it's safer there. You go get the geology degree I didn't." Josh swallowed, as he heard more mortars shake the building. "See y'all, Bro. This may be it for me." He clicked off his phone; felt debris hit the tears on his cheeks, and closed his eyes. *Is this it?*

The next thing he knew, the loudspeaker jolted him awake with an English voice. "This is Rachel at the switchboard. Lieutenant Isaacson, you have an overseas telephone call. Turn your radio on so that Radio-Ops can open your line."

Josh reset his radiophone.

"Joshua, are you all right?" Estee Isaacson's overseas Southern voice was thick with concern.

"Mom—? Yeah, sure."

"*Mazel tov.* He's talking to us." Dr. Dan Isaacson, Josh's father, shouted from an extension phone.

Twelve-year-old sister Julie piped up. "They say you're a hero."

Josh took a breath. *The family's on the phone to congratulate the killer. It's not like Bro to rat on me.* "Junior around?"

"Joshua, the hospital says you're on the critical list," Estee answered. "Junior's downtown at college. I couldn't sleep last night worrying."

"They shifted us from your barracks at Tzrifin to the Rose of Sharon," Dan's comforting baritone voice took over. "That's the city hospital in the Yafo district. Someone said you fought yesterday. The Western world should give you a medal, Joshua, if they only knew you're saving them."

"Right on, Dad —" Irony mixed with fear crept into Josh's voice.

"I never should have let you go to Israel," Estee choked, imagining her good-looking son on a military cot. "You are an American first, a Jew second."

"Then you never should have let some Arabs bomb the World Trade Center, Mom."

"Charleston to Atlanta to Tel Aviv. We made reservations. We're coming right over to bring you home."

"Don't come, Mom. They exaggerate this critical thing here."

"Your voice doesn't sound quite like you," Dan persisted. "Are you handling things, okay?"

"Sure I am, Dad." A mortar rocked the ceiling sending his gurney skidding into a swaying wall. "Don't fly over now. I'll call you soon." Josh released the talk button. *They're so alive. So intuitive. They can tell by my voice I'm not handling what's going on. Just one last time I wanted to hear them.*

The stabbing pain held back during his phone calls flooded his mind. He pressed the call button again and pushed his entire Carolina accent into his voice. "Nurse? Rachel, anybody—y'all gotta get me a shot."

"No doctors or nurses can leave their stations, Lieutenant," Rachel answered in English, "You better pray."

"I need a painkiller. I don't need a prayer."

He slid a thumb off the intercom, and gritted his teeth. He grabbed his radiophone in anger and raised it to the level of his eyes. *The family will call me constantly now. I'm a man, now. Have to handle this on my own.* He saw a waste container a few feet away. *Good-bye, Western civilization.* He lobbed the phone into the basket. Nerves crackled in his forehead. Shocks from yesterday's tunnel fight spread through his body, and to brace himself he clenched the gurney's iron frame. *Nurse Tarcai said secondary sound concussions could crack my ribs or damage my heart, but can be of short duration. I must hang on... 'Hear O Israel, the Lord our God, the Lord is one'... I've lost the right to pray.*

He heard the murmuring song he had heard earlier in the corridor. "Someone there?" His voice was a croak. *Every part of me is fading away. A molecule of me is all that's alive. I'm going to die young in a foreign country. Me, with fancy plans to make cities rise in the world's wastelands. Why did God send me here to be wasted?*

Again, Josh heard humming sounds. A rhythmic Israeli melody.

Da—dada da da da da da—da dada...
Mmm—mamum ma ma ma ma—ma mamum...

Da—dada da da da da da—da dada…

The honeyed voice sounded a million miles from the hospital and from all his cares.. A picture floated into his head; kids singing the lament "On Top of Old Smoky." *A campfire under a yellow moon. Carefree Camp, in the woods near our first home in Liberty Hill, in northern South Carolina. Why did we ever grow up?*

The mysterious singing voice carried him high, higher, until he slipped out of his conscious mind. Creases of fright and agony in his face relaxed. His tremors shuddered silent. The vise of pain holding his body dissolved. He fell into exhausted sleep.

chapter two

Afternoon, Friday, March 19, as humid air blew through Sharon's broken windows…

Josh awoke to the smell of sardines from the processing plant down the hill at Jaffa's port harbor. Rachel's cheerful voice sounded on the intercom. He opened his eyes. Balmy Mediterranean winds tousled his sandy hair. Groggy, he put on his glasses and looked around. He was stretched flat on top of his bed. Overhead, an IV stand fed plastic tubes down to his arms and beside him an EKG machine monitored his vitals. Nurse Tarcai sat in her green scrubs atop a high stool. *I'm back in my fourth floor hospital room and Israel is keeping me alive.*

"Is it still Thursday, Miz Tarcai?" Josh forgot to speak Hebrew.

"You've had a good day's snooze. It's bloody late on Friday, my hero." Carol Ann Tarcai spoke English with a strong, decidedly Irish lilt. Plump, well-curved, and fortyish, she wore a sensitive, troubled but kind face and kept her far-sighted tortoise shell glasses on top of her head, tucked into her brown curly hair. She bent over a stainless steel rolling table, opened packages of laparoscopy pack dressings, pickup tongs and other instruments. Then, she started to pull on sterile gloves.

"What are y'all doing?" Josh asked. Under pressure, his childhood drawl took over.

Carol Ann locked the calibrated wheel of her microscope. "Helping you trim your tummy swell, boyo." While her warm voice showed concern for Josh, she never glanced from her work. Undoing the shoelace dressings, and using the pickups, she proceeded with the absorbent gauze towels to débride the wound.

"Sure, when I changed your laps last night you never moved a muscle ... " With grimacing distaste deepening the creases in her face, she clamped onto a soiled lap that held purplish flesh embedded with metal shards, nails, and ball bearings. "This afternoon, you'll feel no more than a splinter waving good-bye to a thumb." She pulled the dressing out of his stomach.

Josh screamed, his upper body heaving upwards in pain. "Are y'all kidding?" The stench of rotten eggs rising from his blue-colored hamburger flesh gagged him.

"Two days," Josh shuddered, wrenching with nausea, "Am I still chock-full of decayed tissue?"

"Your whole abdomen was trashed by the shrapnel. I'm sorry for your pain. I gave you a big hit of morphine." Carol Ann dropped the bloodied lap pads into a pan. "Only barbarians raid a hospital to inflict more suffering on sick people." She squinted through the scope and steered her scissors and forceps to peel the necrotic cells away from the healthy tissue. "The lap packs are doing their work, absorbing fluids and drying up the pus to avoid serious infection. Surgery is backed up today with emergencies from the attack yesterday, but you're scheduled early tomorrow morning for FBR."

"Y'all tell me, what's that?" Eyes shut; Josh grimaced as the pincers probed his wound.

"Foreign bodies removal. I'll not hurt the brave officer if he keeps talking Southern … "

"It's as good as your Irish English," Josh winced.

Gently, Carol Ann withdrew a third encrusted clump of dead tissue.

A twitch began to seize Josh's body. Hastily, the nurse let go of the forceps and pressed down on the soldier's legs.

"Morphine—" Josh begged. The trauma cramped his stomach with excruciating force. His eyes opened wide in terror. "Morphine." He clutched the bed's frame, the nails of his fingers burning white.

Carol Ann glanced at the EKG screen. "Sorry, Yankee lad."

"I'm in agony!"

"Four hours more to morphine." With all the force in her, Carol Ann pushed down to break the tremble along the muscles.

"Please—"

"Pray, Lieutenant."

"I can't pray! The first chapter of Genesis, 'God created man in his own image –' I just killed five people." Josh's body writhed. "Listen, Miz Tarcai, when I was down in the basement during the shelling I heard a nurse singing—"

"While we were under attack, a nurse sang?" Carol Ann looked incredulous.

"Her voice was cool. I forgot about the pain somehow and

fell asleep. Can you plead with that gal to come up here so I can get through tonight?"

"Yesterday was a fright, a nightmare. Patients and personnel were everywhere." The grim-faced nurse shook her head in despair. "No way do I know how to trace your angel of mercy."

"For a Southerner, who came here to change the world, please?" Josh managed a raised eyebrow and a mocking grin. "For a young soldier, off to the basement in the morning for life or death surgery?"

Carol Ann watched the quiver through the lieutenant's legs and chest finally begin to subside under the pressure of her hands. She started to push her portable table toward the door. Her mind plummeted into its familiar depression, sucking at her physical energy. Another black whirlpool, she warned herself helplessly. *The terrorist attack is having its effect on a refugee's psyche. I am always hounded back into sweating nighttime fears. Never to be free of dread. Never to be free of anti-Semitism, of being a Jew. Never to be normal, to have a chance at a husband and children.*

Her mind glimpsed images of the different European countries from which she and her father had been expelled. Only when Israel made them citizens four years ago, did she apply for nurse's training and emerge temporarily from her shell of misery and nightmares.

She looked back at the American officer with his wheat-colored hair and freckled nose. *So young, so innocent. An infectious grin surely given to him at birth. He fights for me. For Israel. For humanity. Help him!*

Abruptly, she thrust her arms into a rigid posture above her head. "If I can't find your nightingale, I'll do a high stepping riverdance straight out of Ireland." She propelled the table out of the room, her feet tapping out a saucy jig.

Josh smiled. Wearily, he lifted a finger and made a slow twirl.

***

Later in the day, Sharon Security Ward, third floor . . .

"Getting-better time. Hello?" Speaking Arabic, staff nurse Noor al-Nur, the Chief of Surgery's twenty-seven-year-old lovely assistant, a sultry Jordanian with mocha skin, intelligent cocoa eyes, and a shapely figure, took a dish with three pills from her basket and offered them, with a plastic glass of water, to the mute patient in the bed.

The adolescent's eyes remained closed, her ashen white face stayed motionless.

"Dear, please?" Pleasantly, Noor gently shook the doll the patient clutched in her hands. "You have to fight for yourself. These pills will make you feel better, and get better."

Noor waited. Then, she forcibly lifted the sullen girl from the pillows, pressed the pills into her hands, and watched until the youngster put the tablets in her mouth and drained the glass.

"Noor?" The long floral track curtains around the bed area parted. Fourth floor nurse Carol Ann Tarcai tiptoed forward, beckoning in a comradely fashion to the dark-haired supervisor in a green uniform. Because she was in the prisoner ward and always overly concerned about security, her Irish brogue murmured in English. "My American on the fourth floor is hurting. It's a favor to be asking? Early Thursday, when the hospital was attacked, who were the basement duty nurses? I want to find the one who sang a song. It seems someone crooned him out of his pains and fears."

Noor's brow wrinkled with her customary anxiety. "When the shelling began, all the nurses were directed to upper floors to handle emergencies. No nurse stayed in the basement."

"You are sure?" Carol Ann watched Noor's affirmative nod. "Oh my dear bonnie Lieutenant. It's still hours before his next morphine time. If we could only find that singer, she could ease his torture."

Noor gazed sympathetically into Carol Ann's stalwart face. In those brief seconds, she failed to notice her bed patient slip the pills out of her mouth and ball them in a fist. An instant later, she glanced down at the girl, and then whirled back to Carol Ann. "I heard this girl sing! On a gurney early yesterday morning going into the elevator down to OR. The doctors wanted to examine her again. The poor dear was try-ing to comfort herself. She was in the basement. Thursday morning."

Carol Ann spotted a wheelchair by the window. "Can we take her upstairs now, please? *Go Mbeannai Dia duit!*"

"I have enough trouble with Hebrew and English," Noor giggled, "without your Irish."

"May God bless you, in my Gaelic," Nurse Tarcai's eyes twinkled. "T'would a blessing be for the lieutenant."

"Let's try to get her to say yes." Noor swung her head toward the withdrawn patient. Her full lips trembled with loving concern. "If she helps someone else in pain, my father claims in the name of Allah, help will come to her."

～✦

Sunset, the lieutenant's fourth floor room ...

What a fool I am. Stupefied by pain, Josh twisted on his sheet, glazed eyes on the late day Mediterranean sun glittering off Israeli glass skyscrapers. His mind wandered to a year earlier, when he arrived in this city. His father, through an inheritance, had donated over a million dollars to it. *I saw this place as a Mideast adventure linked to the likes of Abraham and Moses, Jesus of Nazareth, King David, John the Baptist, and the Queen of Sheba. I was so excited. Jews of Tel Aviv and Arabs of Jaffa. A modern city united in 1951 with its origins beginning in 500 A.D. I ran around to Tel Aviv's beaches and cultural centers, ate shish kebob and pita bread, heard the incredible quiet when the entire city shut down on Saturday and lit up with music and dancing after shabbas when the Jewish holy day ended. I climbed Jaffa's harbor parapets and stared down at the oldest port town in the world, its alleys and archways built by a son of Noah. I visited the Old City in Jerusalem, its Armenian, Muslim, Christian, and Jewish quarters. I went to Hebron, the largest city in the West Bank, saw the Tomb of the Patriarchs, and learned Hebron means 'Abraham the friend' in Arabic. I saw the remains of Sodom and Gomorrah by the Dead Sea, floated in the unsinkable saltwater, and climbed the cliffs where the Essenes taught Jesus. I felt I was an American come to spread goodwill on Mideast boiling waters. Instead, I wind up just another casualty of civilization's hatreds and wars.*

Two nurses entered the room, steering a motorized wheelchair with a slight, pale patient slumped in its seat, her eyes lowered. Covering her hair to her cheeks was a *hijab* of cactus roses, the hospital's headscarf issued to Arab women. A green bed sheet covered her from neck to feet. A bearded Israeli soldier tagged behind the group.

"With a supervisor's aid, I located your songbird," Ms. Tarcai declared. "Not one of us. A patient by the name of Haja bin Kanaan."

Noor al-Nur stopped the chair in the center of the room, secured its brake and handed Haja an intercom with cord attached. "A few minutes only can we leave her with you," Noor announced nervously in her college-taught English. "She speaks Arabic, but also some of your language, Lieutenant. We asked her to help you. She promised us to do so."

The armed soldier drew up a stool by the doorway and sat down. Josh watched both nurses leave. He saw the soldier place his M-16 assault rifle across his knees, and put one hand on the trigger guard.

Puzzled, Josh struggled up against the pillows, put on his wire eyeglasses. The teenage girl appeared two or three years younger than him. His appealing face brightened with easy cheerfulness. "Call me Josh, my friends do."

Haja stared at the first American she had ever seen up close. He wore gold granny glasses and had a friendly smile. *He's not like the moody Arab boys. His eyes are blue as the Mediterranean and his hair curls into yellow waves. He's a foreign god.* For the first time since she woke up in the hospital, she felt her energy flicker even as anger filled her head. *So this is what the enemy—killers, look like.*

Josh was startled. The girl's chalk-white face contained the fiercest black eyes of any girl he had ever seen. They were flashing at him with rage, and simultaneously held a bottomless innocence that challenged and unsettled him. "Y'all understand English?" he asked, uneasily.

She spotted an IDF officer's jacket on the clothes stand. "You are Israeli?"

"I'm American."

"Gangster, or cowboy—?"

Josh laughed. "Not all Americans are gangsters or cowboys."

"You all shoot on T.V." Her low voice was direct and icy. "Your president is a cowboy. He sells helicopters and tanks to Israel to shoot us." She pursed her wide lips three times in the conservative Muslim custom she had seen her father perform at the sight of someone with blue eyes.

"What's your name again—?"

"Haja." She used the J softly.

Josh pointed at a tattered doll crooked in the chair's armrest. "You got a name for that?"

"Ofanny."

"Sorry. I only know a few Arabic words."

"You know American comics? *Off-anny.*" Haja punched at the midriff of the scruffy doll and laughed as its head flopped helplessly over its legs.

Josh peered at the doll's frizzled dirty curls and red dress. "Orfan … Little Orphan Annie!" Laughing, he threw back his head. A vicious bolt of pain stabbed inside his stomach, radiating out along the nerves of his entire body. Slanting his head to the side, he grabbed the frames of his bed.

Haja watched his fingers twisting helplessly. Before her eyes, the American god turned into an ordinary boy writhing in pain. *Countries and oceans from home. He needs a mother to comfort him.* Her resentment hardened. *He took away my mother. Let him suffer as he made me suffer.* She began to cough. As quickly as the involuntary spasm came, it abruptly ended, leaving her spent and shaken.

"Second story window...over the magnolias..." Whispered wanderings from deep in his delirium escaped Josh's lips. "I saw the white flowers...Mom sang to me, and Bro and Julie..."

Returning slowly from a perspiring, semi-conscious state, Josh opened his eyes, reached to his medical tabletop and greedily gulped water. Staring helplessly at his gold hair, Haja felt a sudden, unwelcome surge of sympathy for the foreign boy.

"Back home," Josh swallowed more water and grinned shakily at his visitor, "my Mom's a singer...all three of us kids play instruments...you have brothers and sisters...family?"

"A father, grandmother." Bitterness flooded her tone of voice.

"Where do you live?"

"In Kharatia."

Josh struggled forward, painfully. "In *Jabaliya*—the refugee camp in Gaza?" Guiltily, he glanced away from her stabbing eyes. *Gaza, that strip of displaced, angry Arabs not too far from the Dead Sea.* His memory shot back to two patrols he had led through that hell hole.

"You are on critical list, the nurse said." Haja folded her thin arms across the hospital sheet. "I'm going to die soon, too. Soldier, what must I do for you?"

"That song I heard in the basement yesterday." He turned back, his voice polite. "Can you sing it for me, please?"

"Aatini Nay? You listened to that?"

"It took my pain away. What does that mean in Arabic?"

"Hand Me the Flute."

"I play the flute!"

"Americans play guitars."

"I have a little flute with me—a recorder. I play it in the barracks." He managed a grin.

"This is Arabic song." Haja spoke meaningfully, adding a touch of scorn. "It's about life having no meaning at all."

"It's your voice. It's your voice I need to hear."

"I can't sing, I tell you. My throat is sick." She coughed, turning her shoulders away.

His eyes locked with hers. "I'm burning up inside. Please?" He smiled.

Her father's strong features crossed Haja's mind. Then, the wounded American with his pure gaze filled her vision.

Josh felt another stab in his stomach. He shut his eyes and fought his fear that the secondary trauma from a mortar shock would shake his body again.

Haja watched his face distorting into lines of agony. A desire to stroke his forehead seized her, and she balled her fists.

I wanted to kill soldiers from his barracks. He's here to conquer my people. He's an American blue-eyed devil. What's come over me?

"I know the American words." Her response amazed her. Slowly, she began to beat her palms together in rhythm. Swallowing several times with difficulty, she began to sing softly, directly.

> "Hand me the flute and hum...
> for singing is life's secret,
> For only ashes remain... after life dies...
> Have you taken the woods as a shelter...
> Seeking streams and climbing rocks?
> Have you bathed in the fields' fragrance?"

Eyes shut, Josh listened, and was astounded. Her warm voice had a velvet quality, mature, and yet youthful; edged with passion, and yet haunted with sadness. *It reminds me of a Jewish cantor singing from his soul. But it's an Arabic song and she's an Arab. How can a girl sing like that, transforming herself from an unhappy teenager into a high priestess of song? She said something about suffering, dying—or did she? I can't remember...*

Singing, Haja watched the pain lines flicker behind the American's granny glasses. She allowed more of herself to enter Khalil Gibran's poetic lyrics.

> "Have you spread the straw at night...
> and been covered by the sky?
> Indifferent to what has come...
> and forgetting what has passed?
> Hand me the flute, and hum...
> for escape is the best remedy,

For people are nothing but lines…
written in water…"

In the doorway, Carol Ann and Noor shook their heads in amazement. The lieutenant was asleep and his breaths drew in and out peacefully. Carol Ann whispered nervously to the staff nurse in Hebrew, "See, we did the right thing for the American." Noor murmured, "I pray the right thing for Haja, too." She advanced into the room, tapped the Palestinian girl's arm, and smiling, released the chair brake and moved her out of the room by hand. Wordlessly, the bearded soldier followed.

The sun's setting rays gleamed on the pearl chair's new left front wheel.

chapter three

Six o'clock on a muggy Sunday evening, March 21 ...

Cleared for moderate exercise thirty-six hours after surgery, Josh slowly hand-propelled his chair down the third floor corridor, searching intently for a particular door number.

The Israeli guard who visited his room on Friday sat on a chair, glazed eyes staring at a bank of video surveillance monitors.

The soldier recognized the lieutenant and returned his questioning nod with a knowing grin, using his M-16 to poke open the green-striped double doors behind him. Josh entered a lengthy patient ward that smelled strongly of medicines and disinfectants. Threading his way down the center aisle carefully between two rows of patients, he spotted Haja's bobbing, flowered headscarf in a corner bed. She was coughing.

He pushed his chair toward her with one hand, putting on his glasses with the other. She lay in a semi-recumbent position, knees up under the sheets, clearing her lungs. He waited for her cough to end. A cut of dark hair knifed low across her ivory forehead emphasizing her blazing eyes.

"How are y'all this evening?" His grin lit his features.

Glaring at him, Haja pulled the hijab adorned with the desert red roses about her cheekbones. He had the friendliest smile she had ever seen on a boy. Even as her blood beat faster, she recited again to herself *Americans came to destroy us.* "I am Arab girl." Pride and defiance rose in her voice, "You cannot come here."

"I'm paying you a return visit." Pure kindness broke across Josh's face. "The surgeons pulled more shrap out of me yesterday." He showed a plastic tube leading under his robe to his abdomen. "More surgery to go, but thanks to this do-it-myself morphine pump, and you, I'm cool."

"Cool?"

"Alongside of me in the OR, were a little girl with parts of her wristwatch in her brain and a soldier in his eighteenth day of spinal paralysis. They weren't so cool." He went on, "I don't take pain well. You gave me two nights of sleep that probably saved my life. I want to say thank you."

Haja glanced away from his eyes. She spotted a stupid Jewish prayer hat pinned to his curly hair. "Your Jewish god could not help you?" She tapped at her doll's midriff propped against her and laughed as *Ofanny* folded helplessly.

"I could say the same about you and Allah." He watched her white smile break along the wide curve of her mouth. *Like a lush wave breaking across a beach. I've never seen that kind of sensuous physical beauty on anybody else.*

"That hat on your head," she knifed at him. "You think it will help you?"

"I could ask the same about your head scarf?"

"Why didn't you tell me you are a Jew—?"

"In the States, religion's no big deal. You don't like Jews, or you don't like Americans?"

"Both." Her mouth clamped.

"Both of us landed in the same hospital." Studying her, he intuited that under her rebellious looks and talk she was a lonely and frightened kid. *And that accusing look of hers really means the opposite—it's her cry for help.* "What does your name mean—Haja?"

"A Muslim girl who makes pilgrimage to Mecca is called Haja. I kept the name since I was little."

"How old are you, seventeen?"

"And ten months!"

"Sing me another song like *Hand me the Flute.*"

"I can't sing now!" She touched her throat.

He grinned. "Oh, yes you can!"

"No, I cannot now." She glanced quickly at his handsome face. *No one ever asked me to sing before. Why should I sing for him again?*

"In the States you could be a star. Your voice comes from your heart."

Haja flushed suddenly. She tried to clear her throat but only began to cough again, the spasm in her lungs turning harsh and uncontrollable. Struggling to breathe, she flattened her legs and doubled over.

Just like her Orphan Annie, Josh thought. He searched for something to help her.

"There—" Haja gasped, pointing at the cabinet beside her. "Blue can ... "

Josh yanked open the top drawer. Spotting a blue aerosol canister, he rushed it into her hands. Haja put the broncho-dilator to her mouth and inhaled large, desperate gulps of the medicated oxyGeneral. The cough receded. Slowly, the flush left her cheeks and she began to breathe normally.

"What's wrong with you?" Josh pivoted his wheelchair alongside her, shaken. "When I first saw you, didn't you say you would not be here long? Why are you in the hospital? My Dad's a doctor at a medical university. He works with specialists and I can call him on the phone. In the States we have all kinds of cures."

"United States—" Haja's bullet eyes flashed. "You think you can cure everything!"

She glimpsed a towering, slender man in a flowing beige *jallabiya*, the Muslim robe, slowly approaching her, his anguished, bony face hardening at the sight of the stranger at her bedside. Haja recognized his cropped black beard beneath the checkered kaffiyeh wound around his hair. *"Neharak saeed, Abouya!"* As she cried good day in Arabic, her face broke into a wide smile.

"Neharek saeed, Haja." Imam Ishmael bin Kanaan returned the greeting. He had thin, dark lips, a sensitive, hawkish nose, and piercing eyes made cautious from ancestral generations that hunted wild game and guarded their goats on the plains and mountain plateaus along Mesopotamia's Fertile Crescent near Egypt.

"Abouya? He is your father, right?" Josh grinned.

"Yes. This is my father."

"*Salaam Aleikum,*" Josh said, bestowing peace upon Ishmael in Arabic, nodding his head at to the ankle-coated visitor. "Do you speak any English?"

"*Ana bihkysh Englesi.*" Ishmael shook his head from side to side

Haja looked at him silently, knowing he knew English.

"Do you speak any Hebrew?" Josh persisted.

"*Ana bihkysh Hebrew!*" Angrily, Ishmael snapped a second reply.

Josh retreated at the sudden, puzzling hostility.

The imam glared down at the stranger's blue eyes, withdrawing a long arm out from under his robe and crossing himself from forehead to heart. He shot Haja a warning glance, stepped to the bed and tightened the hijab around her cheeks.

"Well, I think I'll go." Josh turned his chair. "Take good care of yourself, Haja. *Ma' assalama.*" He managed an Arabic good-bye badly, grinned at the imam, and wheeled away.

Watching intently until the visitor's chair disappeared through the ward doors, the imam closed the private track curtains around Haja's bed. Going to his knees beside her, he clasped her hand and prayed in a hushed, ardent murmur, "I testify that the creator of all the universe including the heavens and earth is Allah. He is the organizer and planner of all its affairs. It is he who gives life and death, and Allah alone is the sustainer and the giver of security ... "

He arose on agile feet as he released Haja's hand. Continuing in Arabic, he kept his voice low. "I was in Jordan organizing a new intifada here to include you. Now, child, tell me all you remember from that afternoon three weeks ago at the bus stop."

Haja's clear brow knitted. "I still don't remember all the details." With ingrained obedience, she continued in Arabic. "Your talk on that Saturday night inspired me. I decided to be a martyr on the Tzrifin bus the next afternoon, because it would be full of soldiers on their return to barracks. I dressed like an Israeli schoolgirl in Western jeans. I loaded the bomb in a backpack exactly as you said and went to the Jaffa Point station."

Ishmael inclined his head with satisfaction.

"Then, it started to rain so I took the pack off to protect it. I saw the bus far down the road." Haja took a breath. "The next I remember, awful smoke stung my eyes. I was lying on the highway, coughing. I remember the air had a horrible smell of acid and fertilizer rot."

"Before you started to board the bus, where was the backpack?"

"Between my legs."

"Any trucks pass you?" Ishmael saw Haja hold up two fingers. He scratched his short beard, inching closer to the bed. "Maybe it was a rock that flew from under a truck tire and punctured the pack. "What have you told the IDF?"

"I swore to them I remembered nothing. I don't even take their medicines, except to stop my cough spells. I'm your daughter ... " Haja's eyes searched desperately for his approval.

From within his jallabiya, Ishmael brought out a package

and laid it on Haja's cabinet. "Situ made grape leaves and fresh *hummus* for you."

"Dear Grandma—!"

"After your arrest I decided the Jews here might force you to talk. I ordered Mama to stay in Jabaliya and not visit you. I apologize."

"I apologize, Papa, for my failure in *shahada*."

"Allahu Akbar." Acknowledging God's greatness, Ishmael moved closer to the bed and dropped his voice further. "You will have a second chance to journey to Paradise for Islam."

Abruptly, he turned sharply and parted the curtains, moving over to the corner window. He stared through tears down at Jaffa's deep-water harbor, and across to its towering minaret and Al Mahmoudiya Mosque. *How lovely my daughter is. When she does a martyr's deed, there will be only my old mama Situ left in our family. No more bin Kanaans to live on our land.* His mind flashed backwards to the year of the battle in the bin Kanaan orchard with the Israelis. The IDF murdered both his father and the sister of his boyhood friend, Rashid ibn Habas. Their bulldozers uprooted every fruit tree in the centuries-old orchard battle. *The bin Kanaans used the accidental death money Israel paid to run away. Dad's oldest, Yasir, and second oldest, Tamir, immigrated to work in Germany. My sister, Usama, bought a citrus grove in Indonesia. She took with her my daughter, my son, and Mariyah, my wife. To have a wife taken from you and become half a man! All of them flew away to live bourgeois lives. Only daughter Haja, who all her life knew in her bones her*

Arab destiny, stayed with me, Dad's youngest and only loyal heir, to reclaim our land of Canaan.

The family thought I hadn't the wits to be a mujahid. Daddy taught that to them. Daddy, whose terrible rages made me stutter, made me lose confidence in myself. But then I read the words of Allah through his messenger Muhammad, and hundreds now respect and follow me. What shall I do about Haja? I must remember that in defense of Islam, there is no room for weak human sentiment.

Ishmael walked back to his daughter's bedside. Awkwardly, he bent forward and put his arms on her shoulders. *How beautiful she is. Her face prepares for Paradise already...* His eyes teared again. "You still want to be a martyr?" he heard his voice waver.

"Why not?" Haja shrugged.

"Has this unfortunate incident in any way changed your decision?"

"You are my imam—"

Ishmael straightened his body. His features reassembled themselves into their usual rigid, defensive expression. "Who was that boy with the Jewish prayer hat and the evil eyes?" he demanded.

"Oh, Abouya, blue eyes is an old-fashioned superstition. He's an American patient here."

Ishmael's slim lips pressed together. *My daughter has been without instruction too long. Away from her grandma and me too long.* "Beware of American Jews," he commanded. "They are copies of Zionist European Jews after World War II—coming here to buy or steal more of our land. Now, in this Jewish hospital, remember to permit personal visits only from our own."

The track curtains rustled apart. "Popping in to say cheerio." Fourth floor nurse Carol Ann Tarcai appeared, laughing. "Lassie, I'm going off shift now. I wanted to look in on you. I must say you have a voice that is—

"*Tetkallamy arabi?*" Ishmael broke into the nurse's words.

"This is my father, Imam bin Kanaan." Haja spoke quickly in English. "He asks if you speak Arabic?"

"Not a bloomin' word," Carol Ann politely tipped her pretty brown curls at the imam. "I speak Hebrew, European tongues, or English with a Dublin twist."

"Men see Haja with nurse always," Ishmael ordered stiffly in English. "With male doctors, same rule for Haja."

Haja flashed a rueful, tiny smile. "Oh father, what can happen to me in a few weeks?"

"What … weeks?" Ishmael's voice was puzzled.

"The doctors said that's how long I have to live."

Ishmael glimpsed the pain hiding in his daughter's eyes. As the nurse quickly approached the bed, he stepped to the side and watched her fluff up his daughter's thin pillows and tenderly stroke her brow.

"As a shepherd—" Ishmael spoke up, choosing English words carefully. "As a shepherd carries a lamb," his husky voice broke hoarsely, I carry you close to my heart, child. Always."

Carol Ann looked up, caught not only by the words of the imam, but by the loving concern in his voice. He is not just this stern, angry holy man standing beside me, she thought.

He is a haunted, sensitive man. "As a boy, Imam bin Kanaan," she inquired, intuitively, "were you a shepherd?"

"Yes. In the hills of Palestine," Ishmael scowled, "before Jews took our land."

Carol Ann stared. *Just like me, a refugee. His voice has the same rage and shame my father's voice had every time he told me we had to move from Bucharest to Prague, to Paris, to Dublin and finally here: Jew and Arab, uprooted by war and persecution, longing for the land on which we were born.* She put her hands on Haja's arms. "Lassie, a young girl like you with love in your heart and a voice to match has every reason to live. Dearie, you must fight for a long, happy life!"

She rose on her feet. With a compassionate dart from her warm brown eyes toward Imam bin Kanaan, she turned quietly and tiptoed through the curtains.

Ishmael watched her rounded body in its white uniform travel through the ward. Then, he closed the long curtains and stepped close to the bed, speaking swiftly in Arabic. "Haja, remember Rashid ibn Habeas, the little mechanic in Jericho? His sister Rashida was shot down with your grandfather by IDF soldiers on our farm? His family owned the orange orchard next to us? He's in charge of the maintenance department here. If you need me, contact him. He is my right hand man. When it's safe, I'll come back to visit, God willing." He moved away, his voice filled with righteous love, as he repeated, *"Insha' Allah."*

chapter four

Rose of Sharon hospital at noon, Monday, March 22...

Through Sunday night and all through morning, Josh fought the pain waves that cramped his muscles into excruciating seizures. It was eighteen hours since the doctors let him roam the hospital. Nurse Tarcai was back on her high stool in her green scrubs and peering into her scope. She was ready to clean his midsection again.

"You're below the frozen area!" Josh's voice rose up. He couldn't take more of this, he knew. *Boy, when the Israeli Army offered a lieutenant's commission, it didn't provide a job description of pain and suffering.* The forceps loosened a hump of steel in his flesh and he decided to talk his way through the torture.

"How come your English has an Irish accent, Ms. Tarcai?"

"I was a teenager in Dublin." Narrowing her eye into the microscope, Carol Ann separated the fused metal. Over his cries, she lifted the pieces out carefully. "Romania, where I was born, is a tiny country. I also speak Czech, Russian, some French, and Hebrew."

"How come—?" Josh wiped his eyes.

"Knowing languages of different countries helped me and my Da' survive."

"How come you didn't stay in any of those countries—?"

"He was a Holocaust refugee. He only had temporary visas until Israel offered him a permanent home." The forceps pulled out encrusted lap pads.

"What about your mother?" Josh gasped.

"She died giving birth to me."

Josh stared at the deep-set lines in Ms. Tarcai's round face and the traces of tragedy in her kind eyes. "I've read about faith keeping Jews and Christians alive in those countries." His stomach burned beyond eternity. "But nobody mentions pain." His voice wavered, and his fingers dug into his eyes. "How did you cope, Ms. Tarcai?

"Lieutenant, when did you come to Israel?" Carol Ann changed subjects.

"After nine-eleven."

"Sure, the American grocery chain that came here?"

"The attack on America, September eleventh!"

"Pardon me, I never heard it called that. And you, a handsome laddie who didn't have to enlist." Smiling fondly, Carol Ann debrided bits of more rotting and necrotic tissue, then changed gloves, repacked his abdomen, and redressed his bandage. Stroking his hair with tender fingers, she murmured. "Go to sleep with you, now ... count friends instead of foes, count all of your joys instead of your woes ... "

"Sleep without another shot? Even Haja couldn't sing me out of this," Josh forced an exhausted smile. "Thanks for finding her. I visited her yesterday. I liked the way she sang, didn't you?"

"Warm as a sunbeam."

"Miz Tarcai, why was there a guard at her door?"

"That's a security ward."

"What's she doing in it?"

Carol Ann licked her lips nervously, and straightened his blanket. "We'll discuss it tomorrow."

"Tell me now."

"Well, she...uh...she is a suicide bomber. A fortunate one who failed."

Josh twisted up on an elbow, stunned. "That girl? Y'all kidding? A Palestinian suicide bomber? Who told you? Failed—what do you mean?"

"She attempted to board a bus in Tel Aviv a few weeks ago." Carol Ann's mouth faltered. "A bomb in her knapsack fizzled out."

"How do they know it belonged to her?" *How could I like her so much?* Josh's head shook in revulsion and disbelief. "Why does she say she has a short time to live? She's not eighteen." He shook his head. "What would make her do something like that?"

Carol Ann's face quivered, giving in to the panicky fear that lived just below her conscious mind. "Hatred buried in our hearts, lives for another day. World War II can repeat itself at anytime in the Middle East."

Josh closed his eyes... *In school they teach us that World War II put an end to hate and murder based on race and religion.*

Here, those feelings are alive again in Haja and hundreds of thou-
sands of other people... Wait a minute. I squeezed the trigger
Saturday on Palestinians, a race and religion apart from me. But
I'm protecting Israel and American security, world civilization,
and law. But Muslim and Jewish laws both preach one God for
all. By killing Palestinians, I went against both laws. When Haja
tried to kill Israelis, she went against the Qur'an, which says that
Allah is God for all...

"Why did y'all send Haja up here, Miz Tarcai?" Josh opened
his eyes.

"You asked for her."

"But you knew she was a terrorist?"

"I talked with Dr. Ramzy's staff nurse." Carol Ann took
a quick breath, hesitating, thinking of Haja's father, Imam bin
Kanaan. "Some people Israel calls terrorists fight for their freedom, too—as in Ireland. We are a municipal hospital here.
There's no discrimination among patients." A determined
look played on her careworn face. "Noor and I agreed the visit
would benefit you both."

Josh studied her eyes. They held the same compassion he
had seen in his mother and in his dad's mother. *An Israeli, an*
American, and an Austrian. And why not? Nurses and mothers
and grandmothers share the same desire to heal people in their
care. What about Haja's innocent eyes—and pure voice? She kills
people? No way.

～

Five p.m. The second floor of the hospital...
Rose of Sharon's Egyptian-born chief of surgery, fifty year-

old Dr. Rafael Ramzy, barely heard the digital chimes as he stared down from his office window. Day and night personnel changing shifts hurried through the courtyard. The doctor's dark chocolate eyes hollowed in a wise face full of suffering, narrowed on the unique, deserted castle building standing in the courtyard center two stories below. With a wrenching sigh, the former basketball forward moved his bent, arthritic body from the window and stiffly lowered it into his padded armchair.

Rafael sipped hot, bracing tea. His staff nurse, Noor al-Nur, prepared it for him each evening. He felt completely fatigued. For three days and nights now, non-stop, he and his limited staff had patched hips, shoulders, and other bones shattered in Thursday's hospital attack. He lifted a clutch of files from the stack on his crowded desk. He swiveled in his leather chair; an expensive gift presented to him from a former class of interns, and began dictation into his recording machine.

Again, the surgeon's eyes strayed above his black half-glasses toward the casement window. March was almost gone. Soon, it would be April first, another anniversary of the padlocking of the courtyard castle. His father Ammon Ramzy, the surgery chief before him at Rose of Sharon, had built it with his own life's savings and donations from hundreds of others. He had raised the money for it, matched it with his own as a medical memorial to the Tomb of the Patriarchs, the historic mosque and temple just hours away in Hebron. His father believed the name Ammon stood for a god of a united Egypt, but the twenty-first century interpretation was for a united Middle

East. Rafael shook his head. The hatred and deadly violence between Jews and Arabs in Tel Aviv-Yafo had forced the closure of the courtyard castle back in 1994. *Papa, so many Mideast leaders and wealthy donors in the States remember you as the April fool. The idealist who threw away his life savings on a dream of Jewish-Arab unity.* Rafael chuckled to himself. *The apple doesn't fall far from the tree. The dreamer's son labors on. Years of April Fools days, Ammon, the violence is still here. Your building is still padlocked.*

"You have an international call from a Dr. Isaacson." Noor stood at the door in her green uniform, her olive eyes smiling at the famous surgeon she admired.

Dr. Ramzy smoothed his mane of rumpled black hair. He turned slowly from his window musings. "In Arabic, Hebrew or French?"

"English."

"Ramzy here … " The doctor's Arabic-tinged English rumbled into the phone.

"Doctor Ramzy, I'm calling from South Carolina in the United States." Dan Isaacson's voice was clear and anxious.

Dr. Ramzy's tone lightened. "I played basketball for the University of South Carolina." Grimacing, he raised his head toward the diplomas and sports mementos grouped along his library shelves and focused on a framed photo of himself in his pre-arthritic days. There he was with the team, all six-foot six of him before ankylosing spondylitis inflamed and bent his spine almost in two.

"I was a goalie on one of their soccer teams," Dan Isaacson said.

"What year?"

"Nineteen sixty-three."

"I was there in sixty-nine."

"My wife and I are longtime donors to Rose of Sharon in Tel-Aviv."

"Appreciated. What can I do for you, Isaacson?"

"I'm inquiring about a lieutenant with the Israel Defense Forces, Joshua Isaacson. I talked to him four days ago. He is in your hospital with minor wounds. I haven't been able to reach him since."

"Let me look in my computer, Doctor." Dr. Ramzy booted up his iMac. "We experienced an attack of unknown origin here Thursday, unfortunately. We've been extremely busy. Direct lines to patient rooms resume tomorrow."

"It occurred to me my son may be shielding news from his mother," Dan threw in.

"I'm reading his chart. He's still with us."

"Can you share it with me, please?"

Looking closely through the spectacles perched on his nose, Dr. Ramzy read flatly. "Traumatic injuries to abdomen and right leg from foreign bodies imbedded by RPG fire."

"What's RPG?"

"Rocket propulsion grenade. Laced with metals propelled from about twenty meters."

Isaacson's voice swallowed his distress. "Treatment—?"

"Debridement. Each day we remove damaged tissue.

Leaving the wound open against possible infection. Patient hand wheelchair ambulatory to build muscular strength."

"Psychological trauma—? He's a very idealistic college student."

"He's luckier than most because there's been no infection to date, Doctor." Rafael Ramzy was sensitive to the pause on the line. By a fraction, his professional tone softened. "Call my office in a few days. I'll look in on him. Isaacson, it's the end of the day here in Israel and I still haven't made inspection rounds, yet. *Shalom,* Doctor."

Dan returned the traditional blessing, *"Aleikhem shalom."* Heaving a gut-wrenching sigh, he hung up his phone.

For a long time he sat in his seventh story university medical office wondering how he would break the news to Estee.

 ⌁

In the hospital above the falafel aroma from the street...

After supper, Josh worked the wheels of his chair along the polished corridors below his floor. His face was pale and grim, and he paid little attention to the street sounds that came through windows still not repaired from last Thursday's attack. When he reached the third floor security ward he was waved inside the green doors.

"Haja?" He called from outside the track curtain ringing her cubicle.

"What are you doing here?" Haja answered in English.

Josh parted the curtains and steered his chair inside. A night-light shone down on her.

"I came to ask you something." *Her delicate white face is so fragile.*

"Ask what?"

"Are you a bomber, a suicide bomber?" He saw her eyes blaze up.

"Yes!"

"Why?" he swallowed, absorbing the purity of her anger.

"Jabaliya, my home all my life, is the world's largest prison."

"Wars shouldn't be fought by innocent teenagers." His reply was weak, he sensed.

"In Palestine, there are no innocent teenagers."

"Knowing you're going to rip others and yourself to pieces," Josh said, "you can really strap a bomb to your back?"

"While I am alive, Palestinians are dying. Dying as a martyr doesn't mean I die."

He stared, mixed up, and shook up. Worst of all, against his will he felt sympathy for her. Years of his own Hebrew school training in ethics marched through his head. Training she had never known. *God gave moral laws to Moses in the Ten Commandments. Succeeding Jewish generations struggled to live by them and offer them to the world. Laws for godliness, honesty, justice, and good neighborliness. Haja, an admitted suicide bomber, must be ignorant of the commandments. Yet when she sings, her voice is full of love. And through my awful days and nights of despair, her love helped me stay alive.*

"I want to do away with all you jailers. Can you understand, American Jew-in-Israeli-uniform?"

"You assisted me once," Josh avoided his turbulent thoughts. "I came to help you." The magnetic melancholy in her eyes was stabbing him and her righteous gaze of accusation was unnerving. "That's what Americans are about, you know. When neighbors are in danger, we help 'em."

A deep coughing paroxysm abruptly seized her. Automatically, Josh opened the top drawer of the bureau beside her, spotted a blue aerosol can. As he handed it to her, a folded washcloth from the drawer fell to the floor, spilling a mess of white tablets. He gathered them into the cloth, and looked up, watching her inhale. Her cough was subsiding. *She is in as much in pain as I am.* He thought, *we're both paying for our sins in this war.*

"What are these?" He opened the cloth.

Haja slanted her head away from him.

"These are pills you were supposed to take for your throat," Josh guessed. *She is so alone. She's a teenage rebel, the same in the United States, and the same in every country. The same in every generation, turning to violence when parents and societies have become too rich, too powerful, too blind to poverty and inequality. No family member walks in their shoes.* "Do you have any siblings?" he asked.

"Siblings . . ?"

"Like an older brother?"

Haja's head shook sharply. "I have no brother. Years ago, they took him to Egypt." An insane idea occurred to her. *You could be my brother. The brother I always, always longed for.*

Josh replaced the cloth with the pills in the drawer. "Tell me what's wrong with you?" His voice was soft.

She grasped her doll.

"Let's practice the golden rule—be good neighbors." Josh pushed closer to her bed.

She raised her arms to ward away his chair. Instead, their hands touched. A warm current shot through her, leaving her body quivering. She saw Josh staring at her.

Their fingers tightened. Their faces flushed. They both were giddy with joy, electrified and amazed, feeling a churning passion for each other neither had ever experienced.

Haja saw Josh's mouth moving toward hers. Frantically, she thrust Ofanny in front of her, drawing back. "You can't do that," she gasped.

"I just want to kiss you…"

"Haja…" A nurse's voice sounded from outside the closed curtain. "Time for your medicine."

"The pills. Do not tell on me, please!" Haja whispered, terrified.

Noor al-Nur peeked around the curtain. Dr. Ramzy's Jordanian nurse blushed as her large eyes took in the radiant faces of Haja and her visitor. Clearing the curtains back, she beamed at Josh. Her face took on a tremulous smile touched with envy. "I allowed you to remain the last visitor. My boss comes to make rounds. Now is the time to leave, Lieutenant United States."

Eleven p.m., Sharon's maintenance shop under the green-shaded ceiling light…

Methodically, Rashid ibn Habas rolled up four pages of specifications and placed them beside the double battery pearl-white wheelchair on top of his workbench. The caramel-skinned, forty-seven-year-old mechanical engineer whipped off his steel half glasses, stroked his thin black moustache, and murmured to himself out loud to emphasize his decision.

"I replaced the left front wheel. Nothing more. That's it!" His Arabic words echoed in the deserted shop.

"That's our new weapon—"

Rashid whirled, startled brown eyes flushing with guilt.

Imam Ishmael bin Kanaan emerged from the rear of the shop, moving forward with an enthusiastic step.

"No one will tell the difference. Doesn't it look like the other wheelchairs here?" Ishmael waved backwards into the shadows at hospital furniture stacked for repairs. He smiled fondly at his second-in-command of Sharon's secret jihad unit. "This one was made for our special purpose." Continuing in Arabic, he patted the chair atop the bench. "It was tested twice. The chair went undetected. Scientists and chemists designed it to carry a mixture that contains RDX."

"I read the specs," Rashid's face frowned with repressed resentment. "Nitroamine. Sandwich molecules of nitroamine benzenethiol between two metal contacts. Change the voltages sent through the device."

"This single operation of ours will create huge devastation—by far, greater than anything done here before."

"Too complex a job for me." Rashid's tone was evasive.

"You're being modest," Ishmael grinned. "You're our engineer genius." Flattening out the drawings, his dark-haired fingers tapped off the specifications. "You hollow out the tubing completely. Frame, back, arm rests, rear and front wheels. All the spokes, but only one of the batteries. Then, you wire internally each part to the left front wheel. When we deliver the nitrate and fuel from Gaza, you'll load it into the chair. Metal to metal contact will strike an earth-shaking blow for jihad. It will pour fear into non-believers in every part of the world."

"To work on this chair, in this department here every night, is a big risk."

"Risk never bothered you before." Ishmael glanced up from the chair, surprised.

"Their *Mossad* agents ... have increased everywhere."

"So have our acts of resistance."

Rashid shook his head, stubbornly.

Ishmael's forehead wrinkled. "Something wrong?"

The engineer rubbed his sweating hands on his coveralls.

"For this quarter of the year, did you receive your money?" Ishmael asked, pointedly. He watched his fellow mujahid nod, but without a smile of gratitude.

"Is there something your Salima or the four girls need?"

"No."

Ishmael scratched his bearded chin. "You have a problem, Rashid?"

The engineer took a deep, nervous breath, slowly eyeing his leader and best friend. *Three times I swore Ishmael oaths of loyalty. When he made basketball captain in primary school—the first time. When Abram tanks rolled into our part of Jericho and he gave me rocks to hurl. Second time. Fighting side by side with him in his orchard when the IDF shot my sister and his father. Now, finally, I'm going to speak out.* The thought formed deep within him. *My first defiance against his leadership.*

Rashid replaced his glasses and pulled a worn yellow carpenter's pad from his rear coverall pocket. He jabbed at the ruled paper and called out names. "Abdel, Abdullah, Ali bin Kanaan, your father. Batniji, Ebrahim, Rashida, my sister, Garni, Halam—"

"Why do you keep those names?" Ishmael interrupted, disturbed.

"Just our jihad unit." Rashid tapped the pad. "Since it began, I've kept track of names and dates. Fifty-seven dead, wounded, in jail, or exiled."

Ishmael grabbed the pad. He ripped off the pages, tore them into small pieces and threw them into the waste barrel. "Too dangerous to have around. Better not to write anything down." He tossed the pad on the bench.

"This chair," Rashid's hands fingered it, "can eliminate the biggest hospital open to everybody in the city. Destroy many of our few Palestinian doctors as well as many Israeli ones—not to mention all manner of nurses and patients from how many Mideast cities, only Allah knows. The chief doctor here is an Egyptian Christian, and he adopted a Muslim orphan. He too was a basketball player, a star like you in school. Do you know that?"

"Give me a small list—they'll be warned to leave the building—Palestinian Arabs only."

"I have a conviction. We're caught in a whirlpool, Imam." Sharp furrows dug into Rashid's brow. "Spilled blood causes more spilled blood."

"Leadership approved the plan for this month—"

"And next month? Our strikes cause their strikes." Rashid, trembling, wrenched out of himself a hoarse, agonized decision. "Arabs and Jews should share this land."

Ishmael's breath quickened. He stared at his longtime friend. "Are you sick?"

"Because of what we do—you and I, Ishmael—are we headed to paradise or hell?"

"Who has been talking to you?"

Rashid nodded his head decisively. "Someone gave me a copy of *The Forty Hadiths*, our sayings of the prophet Muhammad, peace be upon him."

"Who gave it to you?" The imam waited. He swallowed his temper. "Who is he?"

"A patient here from Lebanon. A Christian preacher. He calls himself 'Brother.'"

"A preacher?" Ishmael smirked. "In the name of Allah, most gracious, most merciful, a Christian gave you a copy of our messenger Muhammad's words? What's his name?"

"Brother Byron. He pointed out Muhammad's thirteenth hadith. It says, 'until we—'"

"'Until we,'" Ishmael interrupted, "'wish for our brothers what we wish for ourselves, none of us are believers.'"

"Imam," the engineer's eyes blazed eagerly, "that shows all lives at this hospital are sacred to Allah. It is holy behavior to follow the thirteenth hadith."

"Have this Lebanese preacher and you forgotten a holy life is obedience to Allah?" Ishmael smiled. His voice slipped into a sermonizing tone. "Allah gave us the line of messengers through Ibrahim, Moses, and Jesus, to Muhammad, his last prophet. Muhammad replaced the dishonest and ungodly behavior of Judaism and Christianity and gave us laws of surrender to Allah—Islam. Through this illiterate man, Allah wrote the final holy book, the *Qur'an*. The Qur'an ordered us to extend Islam's rule, and to perform jihad through the ages in peaceful and warring ways.

"In our times, against Western murderers and corrupters of the earth, who have expelled us from our soil, demolished our homes, arrested us by the thousands, killed our women and children, you and I chose armed struggle." The imam's hands stroked the wheelchair. "Jihad by suicide is our most successful tactic. Besides sowing terror in those who don't follow Allah, who believe only in the material world, this jihad will prove that Muslim and Jewish blood will never mix."

Rashid retrieved his yellow notebook from the workbench and held it up, defiantly. "Your last child in Palestine upstairs in the security ward? We add your daughter to our list?"

Ishmael's grey eyes glowed peacefully in their sockets.

"Haja will have a wedding of joy with Allah. Haja's reward will be a martyr's life in Paradise..."

"And her grandmother who only lives for Haja? When the girl's gone what will keep her alive?"

The rigid lines in Ishmael's face softened. "Situ has lived a full life."

"I choose not to do this." Rashid's hand touched the chair.

With a lightning movement, the imam grasped his friend's hand, tightening it in his steely grip. "You do not have a choice."

Rashid wrenched at his hand. Ishmael softened his hold. Slim body shaking, Rashid freed his arm and tried to rub the raw pain away. His wiry shoulders spoke defeat, but his eyes gleamed with determination. "If it's too late for me, I want my family to have a life. The same life your wife and brothers choose. Allah's love in me is for my four girls and my wife Salima. For them, I demand passports out of the Middle East."

Ishmael snatched the roll of specifications and jammed them into Rashid's hands. Shaking with fury, he rose to his full height, choking out a challenge. "You dare to allow your daughters to live among Western infidels rather than under the rule of Allah?"

Rashid looked up at Ishmael in uncertainty and fear.

"You'll do what you're ordered to do!" Ishmael commanded.

The engineer lowered his eyes. *Give in. I always give in to him. I give in to everybody. I'm no good.*

Ishmael's purple jallabiya flared in front of him as he stepped forward. "Allah is great. There is no one beside him."

The engineer choked his bitterness and shame and bowed in reverence to the holy Muslim robe. "Allah is great. There is no one beside him."

chapter five

Two hours into Tuesday, March 23, along silent, sleeping hospital corridors...

In his manual wheelchair, Josh pushed himself past darkened, undermanned nurse stations and quietly pressed the fourth floor elevator button. On the floor below, at the unguarded security ward where video cameras flickered, he twisted the green doors and found them locked. Frustrated, he wheeled aimlessly along the empty corridor, taking a turn at the end of the hallway toward the half-open street window. The night's brilliant stars shone down and a mist from the Mediterranean Sea was drifting in, its miniscule drops lighting the graceful tops of cypress and cedars of Lebanon trees. From below, he breathed in the jasmine perfume from the bushes in the vacant parking lot. He heard a nightingale singing. Oddly, sitting in a wheelchair and staring at an exotic, strange landscape, knowing shrap was still lodged in his stomach, he sensed the passing seconds to be the happiest of his life.

Involuntarily, he turned. Quietly rolling toward him was Haja.

Josh's temples pounded. "What are you doing here?"

"The security guard at night is an Arab from Jabaliya."

"It's two in the morning…" Josh's voice quavered. Up close, her dark eyes were clear pools alive with sparkle and mystery. "How did you know I'd be here?"

Haja saw his manly face in the moonlight. She felt a sharp, palpable vibration and an urge rose in her to rise from her wheelchair and dash into his arms. Sheer willpower made her wrench her eyes from him. She caught sight of a door with a silver nameplate marked 'Chapel' in both Arabic and Hebrew. Wordlessly, she maneuvered inside.

Josh followed her into the dimly lit worship room, and swung his chair around to face her.

"If we are caught together," Haja murmured, "both of us are in danger."

"I have to steal a kiss."

"Like your rabbis," Haja frowned and smiled, "my father is a holy man."

"Have you told him this is the twenty-first century, a century that's bringing the oldest and newest civilizations together? My brother and I have plans to restore water to ancient deserts starting in China and South America." Josh grinned, leaning his face forward. "Your father can't be against people kissing—?"

Haja didn't smile. "Muslim girls who have boyfriends may be killed."

"What?" Josh almost snickered. "Why?"

"For being wrongly accused through lies and gossip. For rape or adultery. For seeing someone of another religion. For wearing a short skirt, or a T-shirt. Going to the movies, even."

She saw shock replace innocence on his features, but her words were driven by a helpless sense of religious and nationalistic guilt. "A Muslim female who disgraces her family can be shot, buried alive, drowned, or stoned to death."

Hearing, but not believing, Josh sobered up.

"In backward families of the Muslim world, it's called an honor killing. It happens to thousands of girls each year here. Death can happen to the man also."

"Here in Israel?"

"Twenty-five percent of Israelis are Arabs. Thousands more Muslims work here."

Their eyes stared at each other in silence. Waves of hot blood pulsed through their bodies.

Josh glanced around the small chapel. It was split down the center by a waist-high iron railing. On both sides were a few rows of empty cedar pews. *Division, division,* Josh realized. Up front, on a raised platform, were separate prayer areas, one with an open Bible on a stand and a Hebrew eternal red lamp above it. On the other side there was a round thatch roof, a niche in the wall with a glowing red crescent-shaped lamp, and prayer rugs on the wooden floor. *They do have divided worlds.* Josh shivered. Above both prayer areas on the velvet front drape hung a sculptured triangle, its three ends lit in amber, an inner circle glowed in green.

Josh turned back to Haja, his voice uncertain, low. "Why did you come out at two in the morning to look for me?"

"You want to know?" Haja whispered, after a silence.

He nodded.

"For sure?" She leaned toward him. *If he nods yes again, I will take my life in my hands and offer it to him.*

Josh inclined his head in agreement.

"All my life here I was in jail." She measured her words. "For me, the world outside the hospital has gone away. For the next two weeks, I only want to see your blue eyes and watch your face smile."

Silently, Josh inhaled. *She's given me the gift of her soul. That fierce look in her eyes when I first saw her was a pleading challenge to me. My soul belongs to her already. I gave it to her at the corridor window where her presence made the night for me paradise.* He watched her loosen her *hijab* and saw her hair in the moonlight tumble about her thin shoulders. He touched a few lustrous strands. Then, gently, he slowly ran a pulsing finger along the wave of her lips.

She clasped his hand, pressing it until her own burned. Unwilled tears rolled down her cheeks. "There is something bad in my lungs," she whispered.

"If I kiss you will I catch it?" He remembered at her bed in the security ward when she had put her doll in front of her mouth.

She reached out with all of her longing, touching his cheek. "You are my brother now, and much more. I love you forever ... "

"I felt the same, the first moment I saw you." Josh squared his shoulders. *We have just found each other. She wants to risk everything for two weeks. Everything seems against her, against us.* "Haja, we're going to have a long life together." He took a deep, determined breath. "Promise me you will take your medicine? The pills you have not been taking are prednisone—cortisone pills to make your throat and lungs better."

'I promise." His happy smile made her giggle.

Josh steered to the door, opened it a crack, and then backed his chair inside. He retied Haja's scarf. "Nobody is outside. You go back to the ward. I'll make believe I'm saying prayers and I'll leave here later."

Watching her wheel out the door, pictures of his family inserted themselves beside her in his mind. *How can feelings for someone you've known five days reach the same level as people you've loved over a lifetime? A mysterious miracle, life.*

chapter six

Three days later, Friday, March 26, in Sharon's late afternoon heat…

Aided by his hand crutches, Dr. Ramzy moved closer to a patient in the security ward, listening intently as three doctors finished examining x-rays and unanimously recommended ankle surgery.

The chief surgeon's hands gently took hold of the patient's foot, feeling its bones and tendons. He cocked his head to one side as a pianist listens to his own music. The white-coated physicians leaned forward in anticipation. Two had come from Madrid and the third from Shanghai to work as residents under this important orthopedic diagnostician.

"Hydrocortisone, that's all this one needs." Speaking in English with a trace of weary gloom, Rafael instructed them to feel the entire ankle. He had performed two long surgeries since seven a.m., and treated patients during the long afternoon in the understaffed outpatient clinic. Now he had belatedly started his supervisory rounds. "Make sure you give the shot here." A swollen finger touched a precise section of the inflamed location. He added, dryly, "Because you're board certified surgeons doesn't mean you think cut, cut all the time."

Staff Nurse Noor al-Nur nodded at a well-built man in a rumpled brown business suit standing anxiously aside from the group. "Doctor, there is a Daniel Isaacson is here to see you."

"Isaacson?" Dr. Ramzy peered from under his hunched shoulders at the muscular man with pleasant blue eyes and a round *yarmulke* barely pinned atop sandy brown curls. "Was it yesterday you called from South Carolina?"

"Monday night, Doctor." Dan Isaacson adjusted his prayer skullcap more firmly.

"You're the soccer goalie medical man, right?" With a wry, tired grin, the doctor nodded, "Can you come along? We'll talk while making rounds. Noor, get him an ID badge and a white coat so our patients are comfortable with a visitor."

Followed by his attending entourage, Dr. Ramzy entered the security ward's guarded green doors. He moved steadily down the ward's center aisle, examining some patients, checking records, consulting with the residents. Reaching the far corner area, he motioned Noor to ring the curtains around the last cot and to fetch the patient's chart from the inside foot of the bed.

He backed a few feet and beckoned the doctors to join him, including Isaacson.

"Ten days ago," Dr. Ramzy's bass voice lowered to a confidential murmur, "this patient was brought in by ambulance, a victim of a malfunctioned bomb implosion. In our ER, she coughed continually."

He summarized from the clipboard Noor handed him. "Within four days her white blood count dropped alarmingly, but then her WBC climbed back to 5,000. Hemoglobin dropped slowly every day. Chest X rays revealed no specific focal injuries. No sign of infection or fever. Recurrent coughing bouts, low oxygen saturation. General weakness, extremely low blood pressure, malaise. Patient repeatedly refused to talk about the bomb. Analysis of liquid traces in backpack found nearby not identified with known toxic poisons."

Shrugging, the doctor handed Noor the chart. "Working diagnosis is chemical pnuemonitis. Her lungs are inflamed due to exposure to vapors from poisons unknown." Pushing open the floral curtains with one of his canes as he led the doctors inside, he murmured, "If there's further decompensation, she may need to be intubated."

"Maraba, kayfa halak?" Dr. Ramzy addressed the bed patient in Arabic, inquiring how she felt. He lifted her wrist to time her pulse.

"Zain!" Haja said she was all right. She stared defiantly at the doctors staring at her.

"Mazel tov. Good news." Dr. Ramzy nodded in Hebrew. It was his habit to mix and weave languages. He took one of the bronchodilator canisters from the few on her medical stand and indicated to Haja to breathe constantly as needed. He twisted to the onlookers. "Pulse is slightly rapid. Treatment— bronchodilator with nebulizer to prevent bronchospasm. Plus prednisone." He looked down at Haja and made a symbolic small circle with his fingers. He brought it to his mouth. "Pills. Two times a day!"

Turning away, Dr. Ramzy moved out of the curtained area. The residents studied Haja in sober silence, before trailing the

Chief of Surgery through the crowded security ward to the exit doors.

"Let's go to the fourth floor. We can visit your son," Dr. Ramzy continued using English with Dr. Isaacson. "In the Carolinas, what kind of practice do you have?"

"Anesthesiology. But I also research various pathogens," Dan slowed to his companion's pace.

Noor glanced at her notepad, "Lieutenant Isaacson is in the basement for surgical debridement."

"Good, granulation tissue is starting to come in, and he's getting his wounds cleaned up. We have time for tea in the cafeteria. You mind if Noor joins us, Isaacson? Not only has she crossed the Jordan to study for a medical degree here, as my assistant she straightens out all my crooked paths, concocts great tea, and her beauty is a joy to behold."

Dan smiled. Inside the cafeteria, he held a chair out for Noor.

Dr. Ramzy lowered his bowed frame into a seat at the table. Waiting for his steaming mug of tea to cool, he slowly exercised his frozen neck muscles. "You certainly have been a Tel Aviv supporter, Doctor. Noor looked up your donor card. For twenty-three years dividends from Austrian telephone stock you donated have helped keep our ambulances running." He peered upwards, "May I ask you if you have family roots in Israel?"

Dan's wide cheeks reddened with modesty. "With a name like Daniel Isaacson how can I escape Israel being my second home?" He smiled amiably. "I'm from a two-person family. I had a remarkable grandmother—the only parent I ever knew.

From when I was a little boy until I was sixteen, I helped her mail to families in Austrian towns I could never spell right, United States canned food and warm clothing. I was the wrapping boy. And always, she tucked in American twenty-dollar bills. I read the letters that came back. So many lives she healed with small gifts that were priceless in post-war, starving Europe. When she passed on in 1961, I turned twenty-one. The Austrian stock was part of my inheritance from her. I passed it on to Rose of Sharon."

"Why, may I ask, to a municipal hospital?"

"Tel Aviv was a modern Jewish city combining with Jaffa, a four thousand-year-old Arab fishing port. Helping its hospital care for both Jews and Arabs was to watch her money become a healing force in a post-holocaust new world." Dan grinned. "And, there was a private reason for the donation, too—"

Intrigued, both Dr. Ramzy and Noor waited, their teacups forgotten on the table. "The name of your hospital. And your location. You sit on the geographical plain of Sharon, you know? Well, King Solomon's *Song of Songs* was always a favorite of mine, and it mentioned the rose that grows here." Dan laughed. "Well, in my little kingdom of South Carolina, the day I set eyes on my wonderful wife, somehow, in some way I never under-stood, I felt I'd met a rose of Sharon."

Noor watched the doctor's face go red. "Dr. Isaacson, that's a lovely story."

Rafael locked eyes across the table. This stranger's words had revealed the man to him. Squirming in pain, he leaned forward. "My mind's been wandering backwards, too, all this week. Do you object if I confide in you? Your first name is Daniel, you say?"

"Just call me Dan."

"When you arrived on the grounds today, did you notice the building in the center of the hospital courtyard, a padlocked gate around it? It's a replica of the ancient Tomb of the Patriarchs in the West Bank town of Hebron." Rafael's face darkened. "Ammon Ramzy, my father and chief surgeon before me, built it. He was in charge here then. He built that building to be a symbol of Mideast peace."

"You're the second generation of an Egyptian family running a hospital in Israel?" Dan Isaacson was taken aback.

"Egyptians exist in the Mideast, too, Doctor." Rafael allowed a rare glimmer of a smile. "I come from a long line of Coptic Christians. My father insisted we went back eight thousands years to the Pharaohs." His riveting, tutorial voice rose above an ancestral pessimism. "My father was an idealist. All his life, he drilled *ma'at* into me."

"What's that? Dan asked.

"Truth," Rafael growled. "Ma'at was the ancient Egyptian goddess of physical and moral law, of the rightness of things. In today's times, Ma'at to my father meant the entire Middle East, that Jordanians, Saudis, Palestinians, Lebanese, Syrians, and Israelis must be right with the land. He believed neighbors who act together can make ma'at. He devoted his life to put that idea into practice. Here, we treat not only Tel Aviv-Yafo citizens—but also, anyone in the Middle East who needs our expertise and care."

"Dan," the Egyptian doctor awkwardly thrust his muscle-bound head upwards, "Did you take note of the hijab, the head covering issued to Arab female patients, and sculpted above our front doors?" He reached out to the scarf Noor wore over her uniform collar. "Even our nurses like it. My father designed it. It's the Sharon rose you talked about. It blooms in the scorching desert here when hardly anything else survives. But because of the uprising of Palestinian *intifadas* against Israel, April Fools Day will mark another year that the Patriarchs memorial building here has been padlocked, and my father earned the name 'April Fool.'"

Dan Isaacson heaved a kindred sigh. Disturbed, he stroked his yarmulke on his head. "Anti-Jewish acts have been on the rise in the Mideast and in Europe. Like before World War II. We Isaacsons were a large family tree. The handful of us left have many bad dreams. And my oldest son lands in your hospital, now..."

"I can imagine what you're going through," Rafael allowed his voice to soften. "My wife and I have a Palestinian orphan whom we adopted. And two teenagers in university. Every evening, until they enter our front door, we do not draw full breaths."

Dan breathed deeply. "Speaking of teenagers, on rounds today, that innocent teenager who was so badly ill, am I right in assuming she's a result of one of those suicide bombers we see back home on CNN? Horrible that little can be done to save her."

Dr. Ramzy shrugged. "We have many patients in the hospital."

"Ghastly. Awful." Dan frowned. "You've tried everything?"

"Everything we know. Would you research a cure for her,

Doctor, let me ask you, so she can board another bus and try it again?"

"Try what again—?"

"Didn't you recognize you were in the security ward in a prison ward?" Ramzy's strained eyes pierced his visitor. "That innocent teenager was picked up with a homemade bomb in her backpack."

"She was a bomber?" Astonished, Dan Isaacson turned to Noor, seeing her nodding. He set down his cup.

"Don't be shocked," Dr. Ramzy continued, "Israel and its allies have overwhelming military power. But unfortunately, that power has only strengthened the Palestinian fighters cause. They try to level the field by using their bodies. That schoolgirl," the surgeon decided not to drop the hostile tone he heard in his voice, "was a suicide volunteer whose bomb misfired. Since the intifada started in 2000, Doctor, well over 150, mostly young Arabs, have made suicide bombing a frightening, effective tactic. They have almost tempted our doctors to think twice about our Hippocratic Oath in relation to caring for them. Israel is criticized by the United Nations for oppressing the Palestinians, but one thing I know for sure, neither Egyptians nor Israelis send their precious children out to die for the mistakes of our fathers."

The Chief of Surgery began the physical effort to get to his feet. Noor alertly assisted him with his aluminum canes. "Go ahead and visit your son, Dr. Isaacson. Later, I'll look in on rounds."

Fifteen minutes later in Lieutenant Isaacson's room…

Gently, Carol Ann Tarcai readjusted Josh Isaacson's pillows. His father stood nearby, anxiously watching his son sleep. The nurse lifted her tortoise shell glasses into her brown curls. "He is knackered. Shall I be stirring him for you?"

Dr. Isaacson smiled at her Irish-tongued English. "How long ago was his surgery?"

"Three hours about."

"Did they clean out all the shrapnel?"

Carol Ann glanced nervously at the ID badge on her visitor. "Shall I be talking to you as a doctor, sir, or a parent?"

"As a doctor, now. But when Estee, my wife, comes back with me, as parents. On the plane over, she couldn't close her eyes for worrying."

"There is more metal."

"Does that mean more surgery?"

"You have to talk to the doctor in charge. But I repack and debride at bedside what I can each morning—and repack his wounds in the evening."

Dan edged closer to the cot. "How is he taking the pain?"

"The brave boyo was lucky enough to get a PCA machine. When the pain's a torment, he administers wee cc's of morphine himself. He's fairly mobile in his chair. He has the run of the hospital. That's grand for his physical state."

Carol Ann noted Dr. Isaacson's weary face. "The trip from the United States looks like it knackered you out, too. Why don't you get some rest and return in the morn?"

"We are exhausted." Wearily, Dan touched his yamulke. "We traveled without sleep all night and all today."

"What hotel will you be lodged at? If there's any need, I'll ring you up."

"Thank you. King David Intercontinental." Dan handed her a sack. "My wife had me bring a container of their chicken soup."

"The kitchen'll warm it for his supper." Carol Ann beamed, taking the soup. "Your handsome boyo will be tickled pink."

"You are Irish Israeli?"

"Born in Romania."

"We're practically neighbors. I was born in Austria. Vienna." Dan Isaacson smiled.

"Your whole family moved to America?"

The doctor's finger ran across his throat. His smile became an aching frown. "My grandmother, only."

"Only my father and I are survivors." Carol Ann gave the doctor a sisterly look, and then sighed. "Like you've done in the States, we work to build another melting pot here."

Dr. Isaacson caressed Josh's hair and sighed. "He builds our future, you know, yours and ours. Please do everything you can." He turned for the door, and stopped. "May I ask a small favor, please?"

"Please do, Doctor."

"You know that flower headpiece called a hijab, the scarf that nurses and patients sometimes wear? Are they for sale?"

"They are free standard issue from our linen room. Tomorrow, yours for the asking."

"Goodnight, nurse, God bless." Dan opened the door.

"Mazel tov to you, Doctor. Green be the grass you dream on."

chapter seven

"I can lose my job for this." Whispering English nervously, Staff nurse Noor slowly pushed Lieutenant Isaacson quietly past a lone uniformed employee waxing the deserted third floor corridor.

"I haven't seen her for four days. I have to see her, Noor."

"She said the same thing about you," the nurse shook her dark hair. "If someone challenges us, I'll say you had to use the public chapel."

"Say I'm forcing you at gun point, Noor." Pale, Josh smiled, waving the tapered nozzle of the morphine pump strapped to his chair. Distastefully, he gave himself a tiny shot by pushing the control button.

"Lieutenant, are you all right? Are you in pain?"

"Teeny-tiny. But I must see her. Her voice makes everything else not important."

"Both of you must remain in the separate areas in case someone enters. You give me your word?"

"Cross my heart," Josh smiled, and did so.

Noor reached the rosewood door and guided Josh's chair through the dim, deserted worship room to the Hebrew altar on the left side. She glanced up at the triangle sculpture that lit the room from the center of the front wall. "From my first day, that has inspired me."

"What's it signify?" Josh murmured.

"The three arms of the triangle represent the Torah, the Bible, the Qur'an—the 'people of the book.' The circle in the center brings all of us together." Noor's expressive eyes gleamed. She locked his chair. "Fifteen minutes—then I take you both back." With a tremulous wave toward the right side of the room, she hurried out of the chapel.

In the shadowy Muslim area lit by the red crescent lamp, Josh spotted Haja's pearl chair. Her drawn white face was shrouded in her hijab. His heart jumped with longing to put his arms around her. He unlocked his chair quickly.

Haja wheeled closer to her side of the iron rail.

Their bodies met at the waist-high barrier. Their hands crossed over, clasped together, and passionately caressed each other's eyes, cheeks and lips.

Awkwardly, Josh pulled back, remembering his promise to Noor.

"You're taking your medicine?" He saw her head nod. "Is it helping you?"

"I have not seen you for minutes, hours, and days." Her throaty answer was thick with desire. "You had surgery Friday and Saturday. How are you?"

"More to go. My spies informed me the head doctor saw you yesterday. What did he say?"

Shrugging, Haja lifted the blue-wrapped canister in her hands.

She's so alone! Josh breathed in her despair.

His eyes are full of love for me. "Joshua," raising her fragile hands, Haja implored, "I want to touch you. I want to sing softly to you. I want you to hold me." She began to slip off her head shawl. "I want to be free of this with you."

"No—" Josh waved her to stop. "You must protect yourself. I have to talk to you. Things are happening."

"Things? What is 'things'?"

"My Dad flew here from America yesterday, with my Mom. They'll come see me in the morning. He's a doctor and he will help us. I have to talk to you."

"Can you smile before you do?" Frightened tears stood in her eyes. "I live for your smile, now."

"Noor's only given us fifteen minutes here," Josh managed a grin, and spoke slowly. "You know, my father, Daniel Isaacson, is a very religious man. He's what is called orthodox, like an Islamist. His family included East European bankers with lots of uncles and aunts. Nazis in World War II hunted down twenty-six Isaacsons. Exterminated, just because they held the name."

Josh drew in air. "My father's grandmother managed to escape and took him to South Carolina in America where she raised him. Dan, his grandmother, and my Mom gave me a home, an education, wisdom, cultural values, and love. I learned Jewish history, the teachings from the Torah—similar to the Qur'an—honoring Allah by doing a daily good deed."

Josh stopped. "Now—" his straightforward gaze pled his case, "how can I tell my dad and mom that I'm crazy about … a suicide bomber … who kills Jews? Let me tell them your actions were just a terrible mistake?"

Haja shrank back against her chair. Josh leaned forward, whispering. "Your eyes are the windows to your soul. Your voice is the music of your soul. I listen to you sing. You cannot have a killer's soul. On that, I bet my life!"

Haja lifted her head. "You are in front of me by how many?"

"What do you mean? How many what?"

Her voice was ice-hard. "How many of my people did you kill in the tunnel?"

"In what tunnel?"

"Two Wednesdays ago in Rafah Tunnel under the Gaza border?"

"Who told you about that?" Josh paled.

"It's not only your side that has spies. You killed five people. Are you angry with yourself? Or the Israelis you serve?"

"Smugglers in the tunnel," Josh replied earnestly, "were bringing in rocket launchers, missiles and ammunition. I tried to help stop people from killing each other."

"By the murder of our side."

"Your side should not bring in boxes of guns and ammo."

"The Jews take our land. They kill us and imprison us when we fight for it!"

"My father doesn't take your land!" Josh's tone escalated "He's Jewish."

Noor slipped into the chapel, unnoticed, and hastily shut the door.

Haja's voice rose. "You Americans gives Israel tanks and planes."

"Shh—" Noor warned Haja.

"Our side has only their bodies to turn into bombs!" Haja continued.

"People," Josh spoke out, "who think God rewards them for killing themselves and others are crazies."

"Shh!" Noor's eyes enlarged with fear. "Both of you."

"Noor, take me back." Haja spun her chair toward the door. "I am not a crazy!"

"You both said you were crazy for each other," Noor panicked. "Why are you fighting?"

"You are not crazy?" Josh demanded of Haja. "Suppose you were not crazy, not a bomber, would you still like me? Suppose I was not American, and not a Jew, would you still feel for me like I feel for you?"

For a second, Haja slowed, puzzled. Her core beliefs hardened her face. "You're the one crazy." She reached for the doorknob.

"Please, both of you!" Noor flung her arms toward the triangle and circle sculpture glowing on the dark front wall. "This room is for healing!" She turned. Haja was already opening the door. The nurse threw a cautionary glance to the American. "I'll be right back for you." She ran after Haja.

Alone, Josh touched his forehead. It felt feverish and sweaty. Confused, he began to shiver.

Lt. Isaacson's fourth floor room, after breakfast...

"Mom and Dad!" Josh waved from his bed. He watched his parents sidestep a nurse and cleaning man to enter his room.

Estee Isaacson faltered, a knot beginning to clutch inside her. She took in the IV stand, EKG monitor, and the console piled with gauze pads and medicines.

"Welcome to the Rose of Sharon." Grinning, Josh pushed away an untouched food tray. Self-consciously, he raised himself on his elbows.

"Joshua, honey..." *Good Lord, how thin he is!* Estee hugged her son and kissed his cheeks. Stylish and attractive, with a greenish tint to her light brown eyes, the pregnant, forty-three year-old mother of three wore a yellow Dior dress and matching straw hat.

"Mother." Josh untangled himself from her curling, long black hair. Her magnetic presence, and her familiar gardenia fragrance, forced him to fight for manly self-control. "Thanks for the great soup last night, Mom."

"The 'King David' makes the best chicken soup in Israel. The chef's from the Stage Delicatessen in Atlanta, Dan found out." Estee forced a laugh. "Honey, you seem hot. Daniel, feel his head."

His father gave Josh an emotional embrace, and then felt his forehead. He nodded his head slightly.

"How are Junior and Julie?"

"Your brother and sister send all their love to their hero. So does the new about-to-be addition to the family." Estee clasped her hands over her slightly rounded stomach and put on a smile. "So, will you be promoted to captain?"

Josh dismissed the question with the shake of his head.

"We all have been calling your cell phone without an answer—"

"I threw it away ... "

"Did you? Why?" Estee put out a hand to his bed.

Josh turned to his father. "Doc—how was the flight from Atlanta?"

"Fine. Mazel tov on your military action. When more terrorists are killed around the world, we'll all have peace."

"What do the doctors say about you, Joshua?" Accidentally, Estee's hand brushed against his body. As a knife of pain convulsed and agonized him, she raised her shopping bag to hide her face. "I'll find a nurse to take care of these for you." Shaking, she rose to her tall height, "Honey, I found fresh grapes and more soup for you." Unnerved, tears flooding her eyes, she disappeared quickly out the door.

Josh stared after her. "Doc, you shouldn't have let Mom make the trip. The Middle East's not a place for a pregnant lady. She belongs back in her garden."

"Don't sell Estee short. Her parents named her after Queen Esther—remember? She blames herself and me, our generation, for your being here." Dan sighed. "How difficult is all this for you, son?"

"I killed some kids, you know, hardly older then Junior and Julie."

"You feeling remorse?"

"Of course. Disillusionment, too." Gaza's stinking, fearful Rafah Tunnel crashed into Josh's mind. He watched himself shooting at screaming shadows. "Thou shalt not kill. You taught me the sixth commandment, Dad. I disobeyed it."

"Do you reason with people who want to drive you into the Mediterranean? Do you believe innocents should be murdered because they board a bus, or because they happen to be born as Jews?"

Dan went on. "Jews in my father's generation, Josh, went down before Nazi animals without much of a fight. In Britain and the States and the new coalition countries of the willing, yours is a fighting generation, fighting for the future against Arabs behaving as animals."

How can I tell him? Josh looked at the man he idolized and respected. *How can I tell him about Haja and ask him to save her life?*

～⭒

Inside the hospital maintenance department in the evening's velvet heat...

Engineer Rashid ibn Habas climbed down his stepladder with reluctance, bringing a pneumatic tire out of hiding. He laid the wheel next to the disassembled chair. Speaking Arabic, he announced, reluctantly, "One set of spokes is hollowed out."

"Only one wheel?" In his floor-length white jallabiya, Ishmael leaned over the green-shaded workbench, inspecting it.

"Hospital repairs keep me too busy." Rashid's tone was defensive.

With growing admiration, Ishmael squinted through the concave wheelchair spokes. "On our farm, I know why Dad called you every spring to overhaul every machine...perfect!...perfect." His words in Arabic dropped lower, even as he glanced around the deserted shop to make doubly sure he and Rashid were alone. "The RDX powder is on a Saudi tanker. It's coming up the Red Sea to the Jordan border. The fertilizer's already at our Gaza lab. We're doing the chemical compression, making a very light liquid. When you pack it into the frame and into only one battery, remember—the weight will be the same as now. No one will notice."

The imam straightened to his full height. "Tomorrow, on Sunday, fuel shipment will be made to you in an Israeli truck full of hospital soap detergents."

"That's not safe." Rashid's bowed head shook from side to side.

"It is more likely that an Arab truck would be refused at a checkpoint during weekdays." Ishmael reasoned. "Or searched with extra inspectors when they unload here. You are to pack the chair immediately. I'll return soon for a final inspection." Ishmael patted the wheelchair. "When it's loaded, how much of the hospital do you figure it will destroy?"

Rashid wiped at his coveralls. "You read the specs same as I did."

"You're the expert on explosions."

"Five floors, for sure. Kiosks and buildings in the neighborhood will also collapse."

"Afterwards," Ishmael's voice wavered slightly, "will there be any trace of the chair?"

"The chair will turn into a fireball—and then evaporate. So will many people—including Haja."

Ishmael's lips tightened involuntarily. He nodded.

Rashid's head rose, his eyes narrowing into slits. "Why do you think Israelis don't send their teenagers to do suicide bombings?"

"They do not have our faith in martyrdom, in paradise, in Allah. They are overfed, decadent cowards who cannot inspire their children and can only cling to their life!"

"I say they love life."

"Is this more poison nonsense from your preacher brother?" The imam growled.

"Israelis build buildings, create things. Millions of Muslims create with their lives, too. I say our jihads tear things down. I say our jihads have a martyr complex. We like to die."

Something, someone has changed Rashid. Ishmael thought back through his unit's operations of the past year. *Fifteen bombings, all successes, yet he has turned against the Qur'an. Due to war's pressures no one can be entirely trusted. He knows so much. I must ask Allah what to do about him.*

"Do you know that Haja is a singer?" Rashid added "That an American officer in the hospital says that when she recovers; she can be an international star?"

Ishmael's head snapped. "Who told you that?"

"It's my business to know everything that goes on at Sharon." Rashid pressed on, "Singers who perform for the world make truckloads of money. With their words and actions, they can influence history. Do you still want your Haja to ride this chair?"

"Her lungs," Ishmael stated, gently, "have a poison in them from when her last bomb misfired. In days, she will enter gardens beneath which rivers flow, and be with Allah."

"To die before they live, Ishmael? Is that what we raise our children for? To have only enemies throughout the world?"

Rashid's bitterness boiled over. "The Mideast, America, Europe—the majority of suicide bombers are Muslims. Is Islam a religion of mercy and peace, or blood and slaughter? You preached that every bomb we exploded since we were kids brought us closer to freedom. Has it happened? Our leaders are killed as soon as we replace them. Death, poverty, and misery in Gaza. All of our lives we've been fighting; Arabs and Israelis don't fight for freedom now, but to murder each other. With this chair, you and I will do that to Haja and hundreds more innocents!"

Ishmael's eyes were swollen with righteous anger. "Who uses aircraft and tanks to murder our innocents? Who has money and power? The West attacks the Palestinians. We must defend Islam with all means possible, including holy martyrdom." He grabbed his fellow mujahid by the shirt and twisted him over the workbench. "You have been my right hand! Defy Islamic law and you will be cut off!"

Rashid clawed at his imam, gasping for air.

Trembling, Ishmael withdrew his hands from Rashid. He wrenched his body back under control. "I apologize." The imam stepped backwards, dipped his head in reverence, and crouched to the cement, his long garment flowing around him. He prostrated himself in the direction of Mecca, stretching out his clasped hands in front of him.

"All-powerful and all-knowing creator of the universe," Ishmael murmured, "who brought the world into being and sustains it to its end, here is Ishmael, the first born son of the first man on earth to discover one god, your prophet Ibrahim. Together with my father," Ishmael raised up his powerful fingers, "these hands built your holy *Kaaba* in Mecca. Here is Ishmael, who was to be sacrificed by Ibrahim as a burnt offering on Mount Moriah, but was saved by your voice. Here is Ishmael, whose mother *Hagar* wandered in the desert in search of spring water for her son when you said, 'I will make a great nation of him.' Here is Ishmael, whom your messenger Muhammad commanded to wage war against infidels by the sword!"

The imam extended one arm and ordered Rashid to pray beside him. "Repeat with me, "Once converted to Allah's jihad, it is a capital offense to renounce the faith."

Rashid stood stock-still. Ishmael pulled the engineer's arm down, forcing him to kneel.

"Once converted to Allah," Rashid bowed his head stiffly to Mecca, "it is a capital offense to renounce the faith."

"Death for Islam is an honor," Ishmael prayed.

"Death for Islam is an honor," Rashid mumbled.

"Death for Islam is eternal life in Paradise," Ishmael intoned.

Rashid repeated the words...

chapter eight

Sunday morning, March 28, on the King David Intercontinental Hotel beach patio...

Estee Isaacson uneasily nudged Dan's breakfast chair, but her husband was studying a medical report. Edgy from night dreams of running after bleeding soldiers in a black tunnel, Estee watched two men being briskly escorted away from a nearby table. "Alberto?"

"More tea, Signora Isaacson?" The diminutive, balding Italian waiter with an ID tag pinned to his white and blue hotel uniform arrived with the silver pot. His Roman eyes were tinged with past tragedies.

"Alberto, who were those men?"

"They do not look kosher..." Alberto smiled evasively. His English carried an Italian accent.

"Everyone in the hotel must show identification?" Estee asked.

"No. The hotel is open to everyone, Signora."

"Do y'all have a way of knowing when—when..." Estee paused—an ambulance siren pierced the morning's traffic outside the flowered hotel patio.

"When we hear three screams together," Alberto poured

tea for the sweet-faced American in her long sleeved, calypso blue dress, "we telephone to our houses to check if everyone is safe."

"But there are crowds on the sidewalks and beaches; hundreds of autos on the streets; strangers coming through the hotel. How do you … any one or two of them can—can be … "

Dan, in disapproval, rustled Josh's medical file on the breakfast table.

"Suicide bombers?" Alberto smiled again and filled Dr. Isaacson's cup. "The Signora is right. But right next to them, as you saw, could be our plainclothes police."

Estee hesitated, fingering her pearl necklace, and then blurted out. "Can you live this way, Alberto? Don't you—do you ever want to leave?"

"It is written in the Bible," Alberto drew up his modest chest, "3700 years ago the Jews were exiled from our country. Since then, we have wandered without a home. Now this Jew is in *casa mia*. Home, Signora." His dark eyes swelling with tears, he bowed and backed away. "All the employees pray, Signore and Signora Isaacson, your son to gain recovery completely."

Dan watched him go. "You upset him, Estee." He looked at his watch, swallowed more tea, and closed his son's file. "The hospital opens for visitors at ten o'clock."

"To live in a country, Dan, surrounded by people who hate you all, why don't people just leave? I would do that. If my neighbors didn't like me in South Carolina I would move."

"Where to?" Dan picked up his cell phone.

"North Carolina. And if they hated me there, I would move on."

"No matter where our home was, suppose someone broke down the door and came at us with a gun or a bomb to kill our whole family, would you try to kill them first?"

Estee shook her head, tears coating her eyes. "Sometimes I wish we had raised Joshua as an atheist. Religion. Century upon century, it divides people. Now we have our oldest son in the fight. And his whole generation all over the world. How can it stop? And all we do to heal the divisions is give a little money."

Nauseous with the child in her womb and sleepless from another night of worry, she rose slowly. "Daniel, when we flew over the beaches to land, this absolutely wild thought came to me. Suppose in the middle of the night they switched around the sand in Egypt, Gaza, and Israel. Would people still see holy Arab soil and holy Jewish soil?"

Dan sighed with the sorrow of his ancestors. "Estee, 'tis a consummation devoutly to be wished.' Hundreds of years ago Shakespeare said that." He looked into her eyes. "I have something for you, Honey, a gift for making this terrible trip with me."

Taking a flowered headpiece from his file case, he drew it awkwardly about her neck. "The hospital makes this scarf. Dr. Ramzey said his father designed it in honor of the strong red rose that grows in the desert—a prayer for what could happen here…"

Quietly, Estee ran her fingers over the scarf. "Thank you, Daniel."

"'You make my heart beat faster,'" Dan leaned forward, speaking quietly, "'with a single glance of your eyes, with a single strand of your necklace. You glow like the dawn.'" His color heightened. "'You're as beautiful as the full moon. As pure as the sun.' That's what King Solomon said in Song of Songs."

Dan looked into his wife's face, his eyes loving her.

Estee put her arms around his neck, slowly whispering into his ear. "Do you remember what King Solomon's queen of Sheba replied? "'I am my beloved's, and my beloved is mine.'"

She kissed him, slowly, lovingly.

$\sim$

Two hours later, as a morning storm blew clouds over Rose of Sharon...

Red dust sucked from Yafo's low rooftops swirled through the hospital's upper floors. Swallowing her morning prednisone tablet, Haja set down her glass, coughing. "Please close the window. Draw the curtains, Noor, please."

Her cough became louder and unrestrained. Noor rushed to the bed with a box of tissues and a fresh aerosol canister. In desperation, Haja threw back her head, and in between greedy gulps from the canister, battled to clear her lungs and breathe. Abruptly as the cough had begun, it vanished. Frightened, exhausted, Haja laid her head back on the pillows and watched Noor draw the long curtain around her bed.

"The American lieutenant called me crazy," Haja murmured weakly in Arabic. "Why did he call me crazy? He killed people just like I tried to."

"Why do you care what the handsome boy says?" Noor answered in Arabic.

"What did he mean—would I still like him, Noor, if he was not an American Jew?"

"If the lieutenant came in here now, and you did not know he was American and Jewish, would you like him?"

"That's impossible—" Haja's perceptive eyes flashed.

"Why?"

"That's what he is, American and Jewish!"

"Didn't you tell me you were in love with him?" Noor tidied the medicine stand.

"What do I know what love is?" Haja giggled. "I'm only seventeen. What do I know about love?"

"Eighteen almost," Noor laughed, picking up a hairbrush. "In Jordan that is almost an old maid."

"With your come to me eyes and long lashes, you're so pretty, Noor. And you have, what do boys say—meat on the bones in the right places?" Haja giggled again, "I'll bet you're over twenty-five. Why are you an old maid?"

Untying Haja's hijab, Noor smiled. "I search the face of every man I see, to find someone whose eyes respond to mine. You're lucky."

"Think so, Noor?"

"I wouldn't have risked my job helping you two for anything less." Noor began to comb Haja's hair. "You know what your lieutenant said last night when I brought him to meet you? 'Her voice makes everything else not important.' If somebody would only say that to me, once."

"Time is short for me…" Tears rushed into Haja's eyes.

Noor clasped Haja's skeletal hands and leaned closer. "All the more reason—" Noor took a forceful breath to overcome her own timidity at what she was going to say. "All the more reason to do to your enemies what you pray they do to you. That is what the person I was named after, the Queen Mother of Jordan, says. You know, she's American. You know what else she says? Arab women must free themselves from antiquated laws. Can you believe my father honored me by naming me Noor, but refused to allow me to go to medical school because men and women attended the same lectures? That's why I left Jordan for Israel – to become a doctor!"

"You know what my heart wants to do?" Haja leaned upward on her elbows. Two spots of color reddened her cheeks.

"Tell me."

"For only one week," Haja murmured, "even if all Jabaliya throws stones at me afterwards, I want to live in the bridal suite on the twenty-fourth floor of the King David Intercontinental! Where I can hear the Mediterranean whisper by day and at night put my arms around my husband while we watch the stars."

"The American lieutenant!" Noor clasped Haja close in friendship.

Shy tears slid down Haja's face. She laughed. "He is right. I am crazy!"

"When love does not contain madness, it is not love," Noor giggled. Her beeper sounded. She lifted her cell phone from her uniform pocket, listened, and then replied in crisp Hebrew. "I'll meet you in his room, Dr. Ramzy." Straightening, her eyes clouding, she looked at Haja and spoke softly, "Overnight, your lieutenant began to lose a little blood."

Noor flung aside the curtain and ran through the ward.

Moments later, on the fourth floor, in the busy corridor outside Josh's room...

Noor heard Dr. Ramzy's calm basso coming from within a knot of white-coated doctors and two visitors in dripping raincoats. Skirting around them, she slipped into the Lieutenant's room. He was deep in sleep. Nurse Tarcai was changing his abdominal bandage. Noor scanned the two green monitors. "His heart beats faster and his blood pressure is lower, Carol Ann?" Noor inquired in Hebrew.

"Slight interior bleeding," Carol Ann answered.

"Has Dr. Ramzy seen him?"

"He was just here. A vessel around the wound might have ruptured, he thinks."

Noor lowered her voice. "Do you think the trips out of his room put him at risk?"

"No need to worry, luv," the older nurse murmured. "Everyday exercises in the wheelchair were prescribed on his chart."

"All yesterday," Noor nervously licked her lips and switched into English, "the Lieutenant and Haja asked to meet alone. It was such a risk. Did I do the wrong thing? I thought—two young people, one with days to live, and the other with a dangerous wound. So late at night I brought them to the chapel. Three minutes later, I had to rush in and separate them. They were having a fighting match about the war."

Carol Ann finished taping Josh's new dressing. A gleam lit

up her sad eyes. "Dearie, they're not fighting about war, but about love. That's a victory, isn't it?"

"You're right." Noor lifted her head. "How is the patient being treated?"

"Morphine as necessary. Dr. Ramzy is doing more research."

"Is there anything I can do?"

"Say your prayers."

"In which language?"

Carol Ann turned and bathed the Lieutenant's brow. "In the language of luv', Dearie."

Two p.m., in the afternoon heat in Josh's room...

"Car-o-lin-a moon keep shin-in,
  Shin-in on the one who waits for me..."

Estee Isaacson, her emotions under tense control, held her son's hand lightly and sang quietly beside his hospital bed.

"Car-o-lin-a moon I'm pin-ing.
  Pin-ing for the place I long to be..."

Josh opened his eyes, lightheaded and restless. "The song has me thinking, Mom..."

She saw he was groggy. "Of Mary Ann or another of your girlfriends back home, Honey?"

"The Carolinas are a fairyland." His head twisted in pain. "So are all my bright ideas about finding water in uninhabited areas of China and South America and building planned cities. The States are a fairyland, too. Shopping malls, supermarkets, super nice people. In the Mideast, you realize every breath you draw can be your last. Makes you think major, major thoughts."

Estee took a light flute-like instrument from the table and handed it to Josh.

"My recorder! Where'd y'all get it?"

"I called the barracks. One of your soldiers delivered it. Play something."

Josh looked fondly at the bone-colored recorder. He was quiet.

"You learned to play that sitting against the pine trees, by Robert E. Lee Pond in Liberty Hill." Estee's compelling voice was soothing. "You were little. Years before we moved to Charleston."

"Mom, I've been thinking... tell me about love, what you felt when you first met Dad?"

"When I first met your father..." Estee touched the flow-ered scarf at her throat, "he could have put out his hand to me and taken me up into the Blue Ridge Mountains, or he could have proposed marriage on the spot." Estee's tenseness gave way to a warm smile. "Love shows in the eyes, Josh, some-times instantly. The heart takes over after that, and its owner is transformed." Glancing down at her wedding ring with pride, she did not notice the stricken acknowledgment in her son's pained eyes.

"Mother, am I still your oldest child or do you trust me as my own man?"

"Honey, that's a mighty big question for a mighty sick son of mine."

"I'm past being just a son. Mom—go to a music store when

you leave here." Josh sucked up against a wave of nausea. "Buy an Arab record by the pop singer Fayrouz, of *Aatini Nay*. In English, *Hand Me the Flute*. Then we'll have a talk. The song is wonderful. I memorized the first five lines—

> 'Hand me the flute and hum, for singing is life's secret,
> For only ashes remain, after life dies,
> Have you taken the woods as a shelter,
> Seeking streams and climbing rocks?
> Have you bathed in the fields' fragrance…'"

Slowly, Josh's eyes closed. He felt himself slipping away. He moved his fingers down the recorder's stops. *The next time I play this… Haja will be singing.*

Estee clasped her son's hand, raising her eyes past the window to the immense blue sky, praying with all her being.

～✕

That evening in Josh's hospital room, at nine thirty p.m.…

"Thanks for bringing me from the security ward." From her motorized chair hidden behind the curtain divider, Haja whispered in Arabic.

"If it's discovered," Carol Ann Tarcai whispered, "that I sweet-talked the guard and switched hours with the Lieutenant's night nurse, back to Dublin on the first boat I'll be ridin'!" She glanced at the locked door. "If the parents knock, we'll pray to both Allah and *Yahweh*, that's Hebrew for my God."

"It has been two days—" Haja peeked at Josh's sleeping figure on his bed. "He's losing blood. I have to be with him!"

"Noor told me about last Saturday. She had to separate the

two of you in the chapel, she said over the dividin' rail between Jews and Arabs you were throwin' punches at each other."

Haja wiped a rolling tear on her cheek. "Nurse—how can you hate and love at the same time?"

"I've never been in love. Noor swears you both are." Wistfully, the nurse tiptoed to the door, the image of Haja's intriguing father coming to her: *my whole life, I always fell for the outsiders with a cause—the strong, willful loners; but I was invisible to them, they never seemed to notice nor need me.* She stopped in mid-stride, remembering, and faced Haja, her voice crisp. "In school I was made to read the sonnets of Willy Shakespeare. The closest ever I came to love was a two-liner that fitted me but never came to pass. 'Such is my love, to thee I so belong…that for thy right, I will bear all wrong.'"

Haja looked into Carol Ann's forlorn, lonely eyes for a long moment. "Can I sing to Joshua?"

"That's the reason I brought you.'" Carol Ann unlocked the door, softly. "I'll stand watch. But sing sweet and softly, luv'—like the coo of a dove."

Haja watched the nurse go. She rose from her chair and pulled the track curtains around Josh's bed. She slipped into the chair beside him. Listening, she concentrated on his deep breathing. Then she stared at his rumpled hair and friendly, noble features. *So this is what my love looks like—handsome and kind—even when he sleeps. When he's awake, he has some ideas that make me crazy. But his pure eyes have stormed my heart. I am his. He told Noor my voice made everything else not impor-*

tant to him. How can two strangers know so quickly they belong to each other?

Praying the cough would not enter her throat, Haja began to sing in Arabic, the way she sang the first time he heard her. Her pitch was low, perfectly on key. She sang with her soul.

"Hand me the flute and hum...for singing is life's secret,
For only ashes remain...after life dies...
Have you taken the woods as a shelter...
Seeking streams and climbing rocks?"

Josh's eyes opened. Haja's hijab of desert roses framed her fierce eyes and lovely face. She was beside him. He closed his eyes. *For defending America. For wanting peace in the entire world. This is my reward.* His fingers found his recorder and he began to blow gently over the eight stops.

"Have you spread the straw at night...and been covered by the sky?"

Haja and Josh made music together.

chapter nine

Monday, March 29, in Rose of Sharon's third floor Conference Room at six-thirty a.m ....

Staff doctors and nurses huddled around Danish rolls and coffee, listening as Dr. Ramzy briefed them from the blackboard. Lieutenant Isaacson's overnight vital signs: heart rate had risen to one hundred ten, blood pressure dropped to ninety.

"Soon after the patient was admitted suffering a blast injury," Dr. Ramzy recapped the emergency case in Hebrew, "he had lost a lot of blood, but his vitals were stabilizing on fluids alone. After surgery, his coag panel was slightly prolonged, but he had no signs of continued hemorrhage. After a few days, we gave him some dextrose and iso-osmotic fluids via his NG tube. He tolerated them so well we pulled his tube and allowed him some fluids. Since he was so young and basically healthy, we allowed limited ambulatory and hand chair movement.

"There now appears some excessive hemorrhage from his daily debridement and his packs are showing signs of increased bleeding." Dr. Ramzy looked up and stopped. Dan Isaacson entered the room, hastily pinning his yamulke on his springy curls.

"Thanks for coming," Dr. Ramzy switched to English, his tone personal and compassionate. "Dr. Isaacson is a researcher and anesthesiologist from America; and the patient's father. I am just telling my staff, Doctor, that I think the Lieutenant's coags are clinically prolonged, and his packs are a bit soaked. We are waiting for new labs, and we've ordered more blood to be held."

"Are you planning to transfuse with packed cells and platelets?" a nurse asked.

"If you are considering a blood transfusion, since his father is here, and he's a doctor, aren't there some things about his personal history we should find out?" The blood bank director, Dr. Richard Levinson, spoke up.

"Yes to both questions."

"What's the Lieutenant's blood type?" Dr. Levinson, a lanky, intent thirty-eight-year-old specialist with a bushy head of black curls, took out his pen, ready to add to Josh's chart.

"O-negative with rare antibodies," Dan Isaacson answered carefully. "We don't really know how he acquired them, maybe a flu, or some other infection. But when he was ten years old, he sustained a traumatic injury that required a blood transfusion. I tried my own blood. It didn't match. Nor did his mother's." Abruptly, Dan paused, clearing his throat and succeeding to continue in a professional manner. "The patient was given typed and crossed blood. It almost killed him instantly from a severe anaphylactic shock. The hematologists at our University discovered he had an acutely reacting IgM antibody that was the trigger. He survived without a blood transfusion, his hemoglobin dropped to 3.7, and stabilized, but he squeaked through."

"Doctor, we have plenty of O type units in storage," Richard Levinson assured Dan.

"You'll have to match him by testing each donor individually," Dan answered, "and be mighty careful to observe blood for aggregates. Make sure there are none. You should start with O neg, M, N, and Lewis negatives, if there are any."

"We will call on our national services center immediately," Dr. Ramzy promised. "There are plenty of universal O types around. Thank God you flew in from South Carolina, Doctor, his military physical didn't tell us this. I am sure Levinson will find a match. I've seen him pull blood from a rock."

"Luck is what we need." Dr. Levinson scratched his head curls, gathering papers. "The frequency may be in less than a hundredth of a percent in our population. Think how many hours we'll have to spend at the scope. Let's hope he doesn't need it."

"You can start with everyone on the hospital staff," Dr. Ramzy ordered Levinson. "Call the Blood Services Center and the other hospitals ASAP. Have them search their donor files for any O negative special cases, and try those."

"Put me to work on the phone, please." Dan stood up, wiping at his eyes, joining the staff hurrying out of the conference room.

～✕

Later in the morning, fog drifted from the sea and clung to the hospital's rooftop...

Speaking softly in Arabic, Ishmael steered Haja's wheelchair onto the hospital roof that doubled as a sun deck. "I'll have Situ send soup, *tabboulleh* and lentils to you. I have to supervise preparations in Gaza. We are going to execute our mission."

The damp air from the Mediterranean Sea brought on Haja's cough. Rearranging the thin green hospital blanket around her chest, Ishmael tenderly scooped up his daughter, placing her in a deck chair. Her helpless coughing upset him. He walked to the low brick wall that lined the roof, grasped the wire fence netting that extended a dozen feet above the brick, and glared out over the red rooftops below.

Haja's spasm lingered. She put on a pair of dark sunglasses to hide herself, still attempting to puzzle through what felt like a minefield. Since yesterday morning, when she confessed to Noor she wanted to marry Joshua and be with him at the King David Intercontinental, her mind had raged in revolt against itself and all her beliefs. *How can I be attracted to a Jew? Against all Papa, and teachers, and schoolbooks taught me, how can I be drawn to an American who has killed Palestinians? Noor told me love is meeting a kindred soul, like seeing a baby sister or meeting a new relative of your family. Joshua feels like family to me. How can that be? I know nothing about his family, his lawless country, and its immoral women who wear hardly any clothes.*

"We will have those buildings!" Ishmael pointed across the shabby Jaffa district at Tel Aviv's glassy skyscraper skyline. Mindful of the few other patients on the roof, he lowered his bitter tone. "Some day soon we will. And the few Jews that are left will live in our crummy quarter."

"Did you always feel like this, even when you were my age?"

"Hatred of the Jew is in our blood…" Ishmael looked

down on his daughter. "Back to the generation before my first father Ibrahim. And after he died."

"Why, Abouya?"

"All this was first ours. Our Kanaan family descends from the original inhabitants of Palestine. That was back two thousand years before Jesus Christ lived, when Canaan stretched from Lebanon to Egypt. Then the Jewish prophet Ibrahim came and bought it and his tribe subdued us. After he was buried in Hebron by his first son, the Jews claimed prophethood passed through his other son Isaac, to Moses and Jesus. When the Jews rejected Jesus, Allah's prophethood passed back to the Ishmaelites, the Arabs of Canaan, and our prophet Muhammad. It is our destiny to rise up against the Jews and reclaim our land."

Haja straightened in the lounge chair. *Back. I hate it when everybody goes thousands of years backwards. Fighting the past over and over. If we all could get rid of our past and be free. Free to love. Maybe love is freedom.*

Unbuttoning his robe, Ishmael stooped beside his daughter. "Watch carefully what I do now, Haja. Practice it exactly the same. Do you see every twenty feet around the roof fence there are light poles in front of the brick wall? At the foot of every pole is a metal plate. This is what you will practice."

He sat in the wheelchair, turned on the power and backed up slowly. Moving the joystick forward, he gained speed, his jallabiya waving behind him, and headed directly at a nearby light pole. He jammed on the brakes just before he crashed into the bottom of the pole, backed up to Haja, turned the current off, crouched beside her, and murmured. "Hit the left front wheel of the chair against the metal pole. That's all you have to do. Many kilograms of explosives will be packed in the chair. The instant after the left wheel hits the metal, you will be a *shaheda* in Paradise."

Quietly, Ishmael removed Haja's glasses and confirmed the unhappiness in her eyes. "It's shaheda—your martyr's mission, isn't it—that troubles you? Haja." He touched the sacred purple kufi skull cap on his head, "Why have I sung *'Joshua fought the battle of Jericho,'* all my life? Because you and I shall turn that song on its head and make the walls of the Jews tumble down. "Neither you nor I can change our fate, our good fortune."

Clumsily, he embraced Haja, and patted the wheelchair. "They bring you every day to the roof. Practice and practice with your joystick. The day of your martyrdom is coming." With a trembling, earnest smile, he left abruptly.

Haja began to sing softly:

"Joshua fought the battle of Jericho, Jericho, Jericho,
Joshua fought the battle of Jericho, and the walls came tumbling—"

She stopped. *I was born in Jericho. So was Ishmael, my father. Here is Joshua from America come to our gates. What does all this mean? Is Allah opening my eyes? To what?*

Noor al-Nur's computer station, Rose of Sharon's second floor, near noon...

In search of an O blood donor, Dr. Ramzy's staff nurse spoke rapidly into the microphone on her chest as simultaneously, her fingers tapped out similar inquires on her computer.

On a corner of her desk, Dan Isaacson pleaded into a second phone.

"Any answers from the Armed Forces pool?" Dr. Ramzy approached his assistant's second floor workstation.

Noor covered her microphone. "They're checking the reserves. None in the IDF"

"National Blood Center?"

"Dr. Levinson talked to them. Nobody. Dr. Isaacson and Rachel at the switchboard are calling all over Israel."

"No matching blood types inside the hospital, even among patients?"

Noor shook her head with reluctance and turned back to her microphone.

"The Lieutenant hasn't got all day." Rafael Ramzy growled. His expression was grave. Head bowed, he pushed away slowly with his canes.

Noor's eyes followed his hobbling body, then abruptly came back to stare at the folders scattered about her cubicle. She searched for a particular file. Not finding it, she unclipped her microphone, left her chair and crouched down before a large wall of file cabinets. In a moment, she found what she was hunting for, the file of security ward prisoners. She hurried back to her desk, opened the file and rifled through the green charts. She put one aside and finished looking through the others.

"Dr. Isaacson," Noor's English words rose with excitement. "The only potential O negative, M negative in the entire city! I found this in the security files. Prisoner records are kept separate."

Dan Isaacson grabbed the card and studied it. "Isn't this the patient I saw with Dr. Ramzy on my first day here—the teenage suicide bomber? She's an Arab."

Noor answered, startled, "This is a non-denominational hospital, Doctor."

"I...I know." Dan Isaacson's guilt-ridden eyes looked uneasily at the coffee-skinned Jordanian nurse. "Josh comes from an orthodox Jewish family and he is—"

"In desperate need of a transfusion," Noor's bright voice cut in. "Here at Sharon, it's standard operating procedure to cross racial and religious boundaries as long as the blood matches."

Dan flushed and rose to his feet. "Let's see her right away."

Minutes later, inside the Security Ward...

Noor drew the examination curtains around Haja's bed. She kept her voice low as she spoke in English. "Her name is Haja bin Kanaan, Dr. Isaacson."

In the clear afternoon light, Dan scanned the patient's medical chart. Fierce feelings and scientific thoughts dueled each other in his mind. *Take blood from an Arab so full of hatred she decided to take her own life to kill innocent Jews. Mix it with Joshua's, whose God-fearing ancestry goes back to Abraham. A boy raised on the intent in Deuteronomy—justice, only justice shall ye pursue. But blood is a sustainer of life. Her blood can save my boy's life.*

Dan looked at the teenager lying in her bed and coughing with an obvious chronic affliction. "Miss, there's a soldier here in the hospital. He is very sick and needs a blood transfusion. Your blood type matches his. The nurse tells me you speak some English? You must answer my questions quickly, and in detail."

Dan walked to the head of the bed with her chart, almost shaking with restrained anger toward her. "You have something toxic in your blood that you inhaled the day the bomb in your backpack misfired. Tell me its ingredients?"

Haja stared silently at the scowling doctor.

"Did you mix the bomb contents yourself?"

Haja noticed he wore a stupid black hat on his head. *Just like Joshua.*

"Did you add any chemicals? Aluminum phosphate? Coal tar, warfarin, arsenic, or bromadiolone?" Dan turned. "Nurse, translate, please. Ask her if she used any other poison?"

Noor translated the questions into Arabic, and then nervously added. "It's your American officer who needs the blood transfusion."

"Tell me who made the bomb so I can ask them what was in it?" Dan demanded.

I do not tattle on my own people. Haja pursed her lips.

"I cannot understand—" Dan's face quivered with rage. "I can't understand how you bombers can claim the right to murder and maim people who have nothing to do with war. Nurse al-Nur—" He spun to Noor. "Tell her she can assist an American who came here to help bring peace and progress to both Jews and Arabs. Tell her." Dan could not stop the tears welling in his eyes. His voice quavered. "I'm…I'm a father trying to save a son's life."

"The bomb smelled horrible." Haja did not wait for the doctor's words to be translated. "Yellow smoke poured from it. That's all I know." She started to cough again.

Dan listened to her respiratory sounds and studied the medical history in his hand. He wiped his eyes and murmured in Hebrew to Noor. "Too risky to take a chance with her blood. She breathed in some particulate that induced pnuemonitis. That explains constant irritation in the larynx and lungs. I can see why they have no hope for her." He marched to the foot of the bed and replaced the chart. A vague notion for her involving bronchoscopy came to his mind. He shook it away. "Let's get back to our phone calls."

"What about blood from a relative?" Haja raised her voice. "Can they have the same blood as me?"

Dan looked up. "You have relatives here?"

"Two."

"Where?" Dan turned back. "Tell me? What are their names?"

"Situ. She is my grandmother."

"How old is she?"

"More than eighty years."

"Your other relative?"

"My father. Ishmael bin Kanaan."

"How old is he?"

"In his forties."

"In good health?" Dan saw Haja nod. "Can we telephone him? Where is he?"

"I don't know."

"There's not a moment to lose." Frantic, Dan flung up his hands. "You must know—"

Haja trembled, torn between concern for Joshua and loyalty to her father. She took a deep breath, her eyes trembling with tears. "The man in charge of the maintenance department knows—Rashid ibn Habas."

"Nurse, come on!" Dan brushed aside the curtain and began to rush through the ward.

꘡

In Tel Aviv traffic, under the five p.m. red Mediterranean sun...

A white bloodmobile with *Rose of Sharon* and blue medical crosses painted on its sides crawled west through the workday jam of pedestrians, cars, and buses. There was an IDF military Humvee in front, and one behind, the convoy had swung out of the hospital parking lot minutes earlier, its inhabitants headed for the Gaza Strip on a hunt for Ishmael bin Kanaan.

"Why don't we switch on the red lights—make like an ambulance?" Dan Isaacson shouted in Hebrew into the intercom.

"We don't call unnecessary attention to our vehicles.

Security, Doctor." The answer came over the van's interior speaker from Captain Ariel Cohen, the thirty-five-year-old IDF officer assigned to hospital security.

"What's your ETA at the Jabaliya Camp? How many miles?" Dan pressed.

The captain's response snapped through the speakers. "Seventy-five point eight. Two hours, depending on check-point clearances."

The convoy reached Highway 2 and sped up as it turned south toward Gaza, the Palestinian territory thirty miles long and ten miles wide, sitting on the Mediterranean coast where Israel and Egypt met. Three men rode the bloodmobile's tan vinyl bench with Dan: Rashid ibn Habas, Sharon's mainte-nance engineer; Al-Jabbar, a thirty-four-year-old desert tan-skinned Israeli Arab paramedic in green hospital coveralls; and a bearded, wary IDF corporal. Dan recalled a *pre-intifada* scenic ride with Estee—the turquoise sea alive with colorful fishing boats, frolicking swimmers in the surf, and a coast road fronted by healthy groves of oranges and lemons. He poked up a window slat. Now, he glimpsed stretches of deserted sea and sand, orchards of bulldozed rotting citrus trees ringed by coiled barbed wire to the edge of the highway.

"Pull down the blind," the soldier ordered, waving his rifle.

Nervously, Dan obeyed and turned his attention to Ishmael's acquaintance, Rashid, sitting slumped on one of two narrow stretcher beds across from him. The engineer's person-nel file had revealed an unschooled but mechanically brilliant native Arab, married, with speaking knowledge of Hebrew and

English. Before he climbed back into his Humvee, Captain Cohen, the bulldog-eyed security chief, had cautioned Dan not to discuss their mission with Rashid. His theory was that the fewer people who knew of Israel's objectives the surer were its chances of success. Dr. Levinson, Sharon's Blood Bank chief, riding along with Captain Cohen, had nodded his bushy head, and reluctantly agreed.

As the bloodmobile bumped over the terrain, Dan pondered. *They ought to know. In America we trust ethnic strangers. In Israel they've learned not to. Still, the engineer is leading us into Jabaliya's dangerous refugee camp filled with hundreds of thousands of Palestinians. He can lead us around for hours before he takes us to Haja's father. Every hour is crucial to Josh's life.*

"Engineer, do you have children?" Dan spoke English and masked his unease with a smile.

Caught off-guard by the question, Rashid's soulful eyes blinked. *Why does the American doctor ask about my children?* He had thought of hardly anything else since a few hours ago when the head of the hospital, Dr. Ramzy, burst into his basement shop ordering him to find Ishmael. He had concluded that someone, informer or Mossad agent, had revealed their plot to blow up Rose of Sharon. Unmasked, he and the imam would pay with their lives for all the Israelis they had killed, and he would never see his children again.

Raising his wary brown eyes, Rashid bit off one word. "Four."

"I have three." Dan beamed. "And one in the oven!"

The bloodmobile lurched to an unexpected stop. The bearded IDF corporal jumped up and steadied himself, his weapon cocked. A squad of Israeli soldiers slid open the panel door, AK-47's at the ready. Grim and foreboding in dark camouflaged battle dress and helmets with purple night vision goggles and mobile phones on their flak vests, they waved the four occupants outside. Half the squad spread-eagled the passengers, including Captain Cohen, and patted them down with rifles and pistols searching for concealed items. Other soldiers hopped into all three vans carrying mechanical bomb detectors in their gloved hands. Dan studied his fellow passengers. They all looked sober and scared out of their wits.

Minutes later, the soldiers reformed on the side of the road. Without a word, the bloodmobile was signaled forward.

"Routine roadblock. Searching for someone!" From the lead Humvee picking up speed, Captain Cohen growled out the words into his intercom.

❧

Twenty-five minutes later, the bloodmobile convoy braked to a stop...

"Rishon Le Ziyyon turnoff checkpoint—everybody out!" Captain Cohen barked into his PA system.

This time, under the yellowing dusk and the camouflaged snout of a Mark III tank cannon, Captain Cohen's military permit to enter Gaza was whisked away for verification. The fifteen convoy members were led single-file past bomb-smelling dogs into a mobile x-ray truck, where they were stripped to their underwear, screened by soldiers in yellow anti-chemical gear, photo-recorded by surveillance cameras, and then sent back to their vehicles.

"You would think an emergency mission would be waved through," the bloodmobile's pink-faced IDF guard fumed in Hebrew as he laced up his boots. "We got a lieutenant desperate for blood and we're treated like Ar—" He stopped, glanced at the darker skinned Rashid and the tan-colored paramedic, Al-Jabbar.

Dan looked at the engineer. *Like Arabs,* he completed the guard's sentence in his mind. *What if Rashid understood? In this kind of humiliating atmosphere why should Arabs cooperate with Israelis? Still, I was told not to tell Rashid the purpose of our journey. The IDF knows more than I do; I better keep quiet.*

The convoy picked up its pace, in spite of a light fog obscuring visibility on the ocean highway leading toward Ashdon. From the bloodmobile's workstation seat, Dan returned stubbornly to his previous conversation with Rashid. "You said you have four children. Boys and girls?"

Rashid stared carefully into the doctor's face.

"One of my three is a princess," Dan smiled. "A girl."

Is this American trying to trick me? Rashid stayed silent.

"You have boys and girls?" Dan opened his hands, waiting for an answer.

"Girls." Rashid gave up one word.

"What are your plans for them? Mine wants to be a world-class tennis player. What are your ambitions for yours?"

Nervously, Rashid stroked his thin moustache. *I may as well tell him.* "Buy them passports to Canada or America."

"To my country?"

Rashid nodded. "In the Mideast there is only war and death."

"As long as there is terrorism."

"What you go through tonight happens to my people day and night." Rashid searched for little used English words. "Terrorism is an answer to life that is made unlivable."

"Why don't you apply for citizenship here and have all the rights that go with it? One out of every five Israelis is an Arab."

"Why don't Jews become Palestinians? Arabs were here before the Jews came."

Dan shook his head, sucking up a breath at the divide he had created. He spread his hands in full appeal. "Rashid, my oldest son is in need of a blood transfusion tonight. His blood type is rare. Someone at the hospital thinks her uncle has the same type of blood." Dan's eyes glistened. "As quickly as you can, will you lead us to Ishmael Bin Kanaan? As one father to another, I'm begging you."

He is begging me. Rashid's resentment rose. *Look at him, a bulging, healthy American with every kind of privilege and power. He's begging me.* Behind his black half-glasses, Rashid narrowed his eyes. "What's in it for me?"

Dan Isaacson's face twisted sidewise as if he had been slapped. He cast his eyes down, collapsed his hands, and drew back on his seat.

Rashid flushed. The thirteenth *hadith* imprinted within his mind: *"until we wish for our brothers what we wish for ourselves, none of us are believers."* He wanted to tear out his tongue. He would give anything to take back the words he had uttered. *Muhammad gave me a chance to be a brother to this doctor, and I struck the man's face.*

Al-Jabbar, the inconspicuous hospital paramedic, crouched aside in the van and jotted a few sentences down on a pad from his coveralls. His Sharon bosses did not know he understood English or that he was Imam Ishmael's eyes and ears in the hospital.

⌒

As the early evening fog spread across Tel Aviv-Yafo ...

In the Rose of Sharon Security Ward, Haja began to cough uncontrollably as the dampness seeped through windows still not repaired from the hospital attack eleven days earlier.

"Shall I call a nurse?" Alarmed, Estee Isaacson edged closer to the patient's bed. She had just introduced herself in English as the mother of the American lieutenant, Josh Isaacson.

"I am Haja. I was on the roof today," Haja gasped in English, shaking her head. "I just breathed too much salt air ... " She stretched to her small table and fastened one of the aerosol canister's to her trembling lips, threw her head back, and inhaled greedily. The paroxysm in her lungs continued. As she gagged repeatedly, her face burned red.

Estee sat down in her beige cashmere pantsuit, glancing at the CD walkman in her hands. She had done what Joshua asked. She'd purchased *Hand Me the Flute* at a music store, and a hospital orderly who played it on his portable player, recognized the song as an Arabic melody he heard sung in the security ward. That led her to the third floor, where the military guard identified the singer as the Arab suicide bomber back in the far corner bed.

She watched the girl coughing helplessly, feeling a mother's concern for the white-faced, arresting teenager whose dark eyes simultaneously held antagonism and a heartbreaking innocent loveliness. Estee felt horror, satisfaction, and then, as she glanced around the tiny bed area, pity. There wasn't a picture, a vase of flowers, any touch of family. Estee's hands moved to her stomach, and she felt the living presence of the new child swimming within her. *To want to destroy your own precious body and kill others in the process, how full of hatred must you be? Wait—isn't hate just love starved for attention?* She watched Haja's convulsions painfully end.

"My son had me buy this Arab song," Estee placed the CD walkman in Haja's fragile white hands. "Maybe you can help clear up a mystery. Why would he want me to listen to the song's last lines? Something about, *"escape is the best remedy, for people are nothing but lines, written in water…"*"

"They are true, in this country." Haja's reply was matter-of-fact.

People are lines written in water? Estee analyzed the words. *She sees herself as only a ripple that disappears in the water. Is this teenager so deprived of love?*

"Please—how is Joshua tonight?" Haja managed an anxious smile.

"You know him?"

"You are the mother who sang to him as a boy. He talks about you. Please, how is he tonight?"

"The doctors want to give him a blood transfusion."

"I know." Haja's face broke into a proud smile. "My father will give the blood."

"What?" Estee's body shook. She grabbed her stomach.

"I wanted to give my blood. They don't take a chance with me!" Her cough began again.

"What are you sick from, child?" Estee asked, coldly.

"Doctors tell me—" Haja handed back the CD player. "I have two, three weeks to live."

Estee's breath caught. She straightened her elegant shoulders, turned her back, and marched out of the ward. Her mind shuddered. *My son to get blood from an Arab? God forbid!"*

She boarded the elevator for Josh's room on the fourth floor. An emergency medical crew stood by the Nurse's Station awaiting a call to prepare Josh for transfusion. His door was closed. Estee prowled the corridor, stewing with anger. It was Nurse Tarcai she waited to confront.

Estee spotted her hurriedly emerging from Josh's room and stepped in her path. "How long have you known about the two of them?" she demanded in English.

Miss Tarcai held up a chart, defensively. "The Chief of Surgery needs the lieutenant's vitals."

"How long have you known about the two of them?"

"The two of whom, Dearie?"

"That suicide girl and my son?"

"Since they met they have been friends, Mrs. Isaacson." Carol Ann kept her voice low.

"He was only hurt a week ago Wednesday. When did they meet?"

"Thursday, the morning after he was admitted, during the attack on the hospital." Carol Ann edged aside, nervously. "I have to go."

Estee blocked her way. "How could you allow them to continue to meet?"

"When he reached the limit for pain killers, her songs helped him manage. She's a born nightingale, Mrs. Isaacson."

"She kills Jews! She is an enemy! This is Tel Aviv, Israel!"

"This is Tel Aviv-Yafo. Patients here are treated as equals."

Estee's face knotted, red with confused anger. "Joshua's bloodline goes back to the founding prophets, Isaac and Abraham. Four thousand years. How dare you consider Arab blood for him?"

Carol Ann Tarcai stared. She recalled ancient Hebrew words that were spoken by Moses. "'The life of the flesh is in the blood,' Mrs. Isaacson. We are trying to save your son." She slipped quickly away.

❧

Under the first glow of the desert night stars, Highway 4, near Bayt Hanun...

The bloodmobile and its Humvee escorts turned off the main artery, swinging east in the direction of the Dead Sea for the ride to Jabaliya. Through the moonscaped desert, their yellow fog lights picked up mile after mile of sand dunes, ghostly charred hulks of vehicles and looted tanks, and occasional orange, lemon and nut orchards. Finally, the convoy reached the three-story refugee camp's watchtower. Captain Cohen presented his military pass and Dr. Levinson flashed the Rose of Sharon emergency medical permit. The concrete gates swung open, and the convoy rolled into Jabaliya's barbed wire encampment. Rashid, had been moved into the lead Humvee. He directed its driver up a winding gravel road. They stopped at a dead end of rotted tires and decaying garbage that jutted over the camp.

Rashid jumped out of the Humvee. He shook his head at the IDF soldiers who scrambled out of the Humvees. Fully armed, with additional stun guns and mace, they were lining up in front of Captain Cohen. In Arabic, Rashid called out, "This is Palestine Authority territory now. If you want Imam Bin Kanaan to cooperate, only the American doctor goes with me. Give me your word before I start. Or else you can draw someone else's blood."

Captain Cohen's steel-black eyes narrowed. He glanced at Richard Levinson, and saw the director of the blood bank nod his head. *"Awedak, awedak!"* He gave his word in Arabic to Rashid.

Dan Isaacson clambered from the bloodmobile carrying two white medical bags marked with blue crosses. He wore a long white hospital coat over a bulletproof vest and a combat helmet over his yarmulke. He shifted the bags to one hand and pinched his nose.

"Your home will smell too," Rashid switched to English, "if you live in a military camp with ninety thousand people and no underground sewage."

"I'll get used to it." Dan poked his flashlight nervously

through the mist in front of him. He murmured a prayer upwards for a long second, and then exhaled and plunged after the engineer into the pitch-black Jabaliya streets.

~~~

In the evening, inside Josh's flower-filled hospital room...

The lieutenant willed himself to remain positive despite the pain throbbing through him and the fear caused by the sight of the machines hooked to his heart, abdomen, and feet. Haja, brought quietly to the room earlier at Nurse Tarcai's insistence, prayed for Josh from her pearl wheelchair alongside his bed. She clutched an inhalator in her hands to prevent a coughing spell. Monitoring the alarming information that flickered across a green computer screen, Noor stood in agitation at the side table. *It's eight o'clock in the evening. No word from the bloodmobile. We're losing the battle of time.* Clamping down on her panicky thoughts, she jotted medical notes on the lieutenant's thick chart.

Tenderly, Haja leaned to Josh. "Your father has gone to find my father. To get from him the fresh blood you need!"

"Looking at you..." Josh whispered, his fingers reaching out slowly, "that's all I need."

She stroked his hand, drinking in the love in his eyes. "We lived on different continents. Oceans separated us, yet our blood type is the same." Her sensitive face shook in amazement. "That's a mystery full of magic to me." Her voice became husky with emotion. "Meeting you has changed my life."

"You have changed mine, too."

"Tell me how--"

"The different customs and backgrounds between us. All the hundreds of people I met growing up in the States, and here. All that disappeared when I set eyes on you."

"Before I met you I was full of anger," Haja murmured, "I had no hope and I wanted to destroy life. Now, my greatest punishment is that I can't kiss your lips. I want to be in the morning sunlight with you. I want to hold you in the light of the moon." She began to cough. "Joshua, what are we going to do?"

"About what?"

"When I die. If you die, too."

"Then our lives will be wasted."

Across the room, turning away her head, Noor dabbed tears from her eyes.

Josh attempted to sit up, collapsed, and fell back on his pillows. "Wait … wait a minute."

Noor rushed over to re-check the wires on his chest.

"This sounds crazy…" Josh struggled up. "Suppose we get married?" Josh's eyes shot sparks. "We wouldn't just be unfortunates lost in war. We would be fortunate people!" He reached for Haja's hands. "We would show that love made war and religious barriers disappear. Then our lives wouldn't be wasted, would they?"

They squeezed hands together, laughing.

"Noor?" Josh asked the Jordanian nurse. "How much have you heard?"

"I'm bringing your chart up to date. A bit—"

"Are we nuts?"

"Nuts? I don't think so," Noor giggled. "Maybe crazy."

"But— you agree if we're old enough to fight," Josh grinned, "we're old enough to marry?"

"I agree," Haja coughed.

"Noor," Josh asked, "does the hospital have a friendly rabbi or imam who can marry—hitch us up?"

Noor's head straightened from fear. "I cannot get near that."

"Why not?"

"The powers that be here would kill me."

"You are named after Noor, the former Queen of Jordan," Haja wheezed. "You told me she said girls should follow their deepest feelings, even defy the powers that be."

Noor stared from the pain-wracked American officer to the suffering girl. A man's distinguished face above his robe came strongly to her mind; a white face that smiled with cheerfulness, even as its sharp features were pitted by advanced melanoma. Brother Byron came to the hospital for chemotherapy treatments. A priest of an order strange to her, he always brought hot coffee for patients, wrote letters for the weak ones, or prayed with the dying.

"I know someone," Noor was surprised to hear herself responding. "He's an outpatient who makes rounds of the wards at night, helps people even though he has cancer. He has some official powers in Lebanon, I believe. Marriage laws are different there, I think."

Startled and thrilled that Brother Byron had popped to mind, Noor turned with a nervous, purposeful smile, and left the room.

Through Jabaliya's darkened, open sewage streets…

Rashid ibn Habas continued to zigzag downwards in the obscure moonlit mist until he reached a forked divide and entered a street to his right. Minutes later, he redoubled back into the dark haze of an alley to the left. He twisted about to make sure only the doctor in the white coat followed him and wound down through three more streets to the bottom of the hill. He stopped at an unlit sheet metal building and pulled away a pile of truck tire carcasses in front of a decayed steel door. Unlocking it quietly with a key, he pushed inside the pitch-black entranceway, the doctor behind him. "Don't make a sound. Wait here," he murmured, and began to disappear along an unlit concrete wall.

"My son's and mine—" Dan whispered after him, impulsively. "Our lives are in your hands now."

Rashid inclined his head an instant and then descended a barely discernable, narrow stone stairway.

Alone, Dan wiped his forehead with an unsteady hand. He began to tremble. Raising his head, he covered his eyes, murmuring in Hebrew and rocking his body slightly: "Hear, O Israel, the Lord is our God, the Lord is One. I thank thee, O God, for the blessings of this day. Thou art my shepherd. I shall not want. I fear no evil for thou art with me …" Hearing noises, the doctor shrank against the wall.

A group of IDF soldiers, rifles at the ready, rushed through the metal door. Captain Cohen led them, his revolver drawn. "Are you all right?" He waved his flashlight at Dr. Isaacson.

"Be quiet!" Dan hissed a reply in Hebrew. "Go away! He's getting Ishmael!"

"We're going to wait with you."

"We agreed I'd be alone—"

"It's my business to protect you."

"We made a promise!" Dan flailed his fists. "Go back outside!"

Captain Cohen flashed his light ahead at the ghostly flight of stairs in front of them, and hesitated.

"Go!" Dan pushed the captain away. "You're endangering my son's life!"

Reluctantly, Captain Cohen waved his men backwards. "If you feel the slightest danger," he whispered, "raise your voice, Doc. We'll be in the street."

In the utter silence that followed, Dan's chest tightened. He forced himself to breathe slowly and repeat his prayer. Footsteps sounded from below. Dan made out Rashid's figure on the stairs, behind him, a second figure following cautiously in a dark robe. Dan sniffed a strong odor of chemicals. He watched the men exchange words in Arabic.

Rashid talked forcefully with his arms raised upwards. He pointed at the doctor in his white coat, with medical equipment at his feet.

Ishmael laughed. He slipped around Rashid, leaping two steps at a time, and approached Dan. He stared at the American doctor, eyes blazing. Then he swept his long arms down to the floor and scooped up the medical bags. English words intoned from his mouth. "Palestine and Jewish blood? Never together! Never together! Allahu Akbar!"

Ishmael hurled the bags down the stairs where they hit the concrete wall and smashed open, scattering the sterilized contents into a cloud of dislodged dust. Ishmael fled down the stairs.

Within seconds, Israeli soldiers burst through the front door, a few wrestling Rashid to the ground, the rest rushing down the stairs, after the disappearing imam.

～✕

Just as the Rose of Sharon clock chimed ten p.m. ...

A grey-haired, strapping, sixty-seven-year-old man moved confidently down the fourth floor corridor dressed in a brown habit tied by a white cord with three knots. He smiled at sleepless patients' relatives on both sides of the still corridor with the air of a contented man thinking only of the welfare of others. Passing a busy employee mopping the floor, he raised the aluminum canister he carried, and sang out in Arabic, "Later, we'll drink one together!"

He passed the visitors' space where Estee Isaacson drowsed and entered Lieutenant Isaacson's room. He saw a nurse's assistant dozing in a corner chair, and in the hospital bed, a youthful man with a yarmulke atop his blond curls. Next to his bed, humming softly in a wheelchair, sat a dark-haired teenage girl in the hospital's enveloping green *chador*.

"I suppose English is the chosen language here?" The gravel-voiced stranger came forward in his open sandals, a broad smile lighting his pale, cancer-pitted face. "May I serve you a nice cup of cappuccino?"

"Who are you?" Josh asked warily, staring at the odd religious robe and sandals.

"I take it you two are the singer and the American lieutenant Dr. Ramzy's staff nurse Noor al-Nur mentioned?"

"Yes we are," Haja nodded softly.

Still beaming, the stranger put down a weathered briefcase, hoisted his half-gallon canister onto the table and busied himself mixing the contents of two small bottles with hot milk. "I was told you want to 'hitch yourselves up?'"

"You're a priest?" Josh caught a Scottish accent.

"I was." The stranger's distinctive burr was clipped and rhythmic. "The Church of England. But I questioned too many traditions too loudly." Wryly, his green eyes twinkled in their hollowed shadows of pain. "Now, I'm with the Order of Friars Minor, a religious order tracing its origin back to St. Francis of Assisi. I'm a Franciscan friar—Brother Byron. Our Franciscan code is 'The Lord gave me brothers'.

"As Abram said to Lot in Genesis—" the brother extended two steaming small cups, "'let's not have any quarreling between you and me, or between your herdsmen and mine, for we are brothers.'"

The lieutenant shook his head and refused his cup.

"My cappuccino is light on coffee and heavy on frothy milk." Byron's grin was direct.

"Thank you," Haja accepted her drink.

"Now let me ask you both a question?" The Franciscan put down the other cup. "How strong is your love?"

"The love of Haja and Joshua is very strong." Haja savored the caramel flavoring with a smile.

"Stronger than the concrete wall the Israelis have erected?"

"Stronger," Josh nodded.

"Lieutenant USA, are you willing to convert to the Muslim faith to marry?"

Josh blinked his eyes.

"You must do that..." Brother Byron smiled broadly at the pretty girl in the wheelchair, "unless you agree to convert to Judaism?"

Haja slowly shook her head.

"We can't leave our religions." Josh declared. "We can't hurt our families."

"Then your love is not stronger than your religious beliefs and your feelings for your parents?" The friar glanced from one to the other. He spoke gently into their silence. "Then I cannot help you."

"I haven't fallen in love with a Muslim." Josh struggled onto an elbow. "She hasn't fallen in love with a Jew. Isn't there a law that just marries people?"

"Not in Israel. And not under Palestinian Authority law."

"Then what do people like us do?" Josh pleaded.

"They go out of the country." The friar collected his things. "I'm very sorry I can't help you."

"I read about St. Francis of Assisi," Josh's words tumbled out awkwardly, but in earnest. "The Franciscans, monks, you help the poor and the sick? You help heal conflicts in the world, right? Haja's conflicts with Israelis are so strong she tried to blow up a bus loaded with them. I killed five Arabs trying to make peace. She lives in Gaza in a state of poverty called Jabaliya and I live in a state of plenty called South Carolina. We fell in love. We want to marry."

Josh breathed painfully. "Doctors give her only days to live because of a chemical she inhaled. I've got infected shrapnel in my stomach, and the doctors are hoping to give me a blood transfusion. Nurse Noor thought you might help us. You're a patient here too, aren't you? Kinda' like us, day to day...?"

Josh sank back against his pillows.

"Yes, I live day by day." Brother Byron rubbed at the pit marks in his ravaged cheeks. He thought momentarily of his own life. "Do your families know about the two of you?"

"My father's an orthodox Jew at war with the Arab world." Weakly, Josh sighed. "I ... can't tell him."

"My father's at holy war with Israel, Jews, the West," Haja said. "He is a Muslim imam."

"This is one brother who believes all children have one father."

"If you believe in that, can't you marry us?" Haja pleaded.

"You know the danger for an Arab girl who marries outside her religion?"

"Joshua's love is worth my life."

"And you wear a yarmulke," Byron turned toward the lieutenant. "Can you face the uncertain future that goes on every day between Israelis and Arabs?"

Josh took in and exhaled a difficult breath. "Haja and I get counted separately as war casualties if we die alone, right? Just two more losers. But if we die married, we're winners, right?" Josh searched the friar's face. "Won't people see then that love, given a chance, can help eliminate war?"

"When we die," Haja murmured, "we want to die married."

Brother Byron saw their hands quietly intertwine, and their eyes, filled with their own sufferings, telegraph love to each other. *Doris and me.* His mind snapped back to the first years of his marriage in 1964, a twenty-seven-year-old Anglican priest in the working-class, dock district of Liverpool. He was an Anglican Scot and white. Doris was Catholic, English, and black—a ballet dancer with a presence so full of joy it lifted up his own from the first moment he laid eyes on her. *Our wedded bliss was going to transform the naysayers in my first parish and subdue the hate-filled stares we were subjected to in lodgings, streetcars, and restaurants. But it hadn't. And after our first child was delivered stillborn, Doris filed for divorce . . . . "I'm going back among my people," she said.*

Brother Byron looked with longing at the two young people. *Doris's action haunted me. It was a defeat of the cardinal Episcopal tenet—God as Father of all of his people. I fought hard for that principle among the persecuted ethnic dock groups until my parish appealed to my Bishop and the church sent me to a year's retreat for displaced priests to do penance. For twenty-five years I lived as a man of faith without conviction, a priest without a parish, lashed by the failure of the world to accept one father as God. Now I am follower of St. Francis, sworn to perform his life's work reborn in me.*

I believe I can bypass Israeli and Palestinian law here, if I have enough courage. But it will be a gamble. I can get into great trouble again. But, Byron, look into the eyes of Joshua and Haja, aren't they fulfilling the Father's law to be guided by the depths of love? Understand their names! Just those names should fill you full of righteous understanding! Your lifelong belief is at stake here, you know. You were not successful in making it clear to Doris, and your illness has given you very few days left to make it clear again!

"I'll be right back." Byron tiptoed to the door of the room and quietly slipped into the corridor.

In the drizzling rain, along the shrouded coast road from Egypt to Israel…

The bloodmobile alternately sped and crawled through the fog back to Tel Aviv-Yafo.

"The Imam has changed his mind," reported Rashid in English.

"He has—?" Slumped with worry, Dr. Isaacson jumped off his seat, in his mind thanking God. He turned to the engineer, saying it out loud. *"Baruch HaShem!"*

"Allahu Akbar." Rashid nodded.

"Allah akbah?" Dan started to open the medical closets above his head.

"God is great." Rashid's handcuffed hands went up and down. He kept his eyes fastened on Ishmael. The imam's face was red and swollen from the fight he had put up in the tunnel below the metal building. He lay strapped on the hard bed across the van's aisle, watched over by Dr. Levinson and Sharon's paramedic, Al-Jabbar.

Rashid felt a great stone lifted from him, even though his own hands were bound. As Israeli soldiers had bundled Ishmael and him into the van, he hissed five Arabic words into his imam's ear—give your blood or I talk! Rashid's eyes watered as he lowered his head. *I'm living the thirteenth hadith. I'm performing true … helping another brother's time on earth to be extended, as I would want for myself."*

"Is this Rose of Sharon? This is Dr. Isaacson in the bloodmobile … " Dan spoke in Hebrew, the mobile phone cradled against his ear as he hastily opened transfusion equipment and oversaw the paramedic transferring Ishmael into the patient chair. "Get word to Dr. Ramzy. We're on our way back. We're taking blood from the father donor. Dr. Levinson and I will make certain the blood is right. We'll see you before morning, hopefully with vials for Lieutenant Isaacson's transfusion."

Richard Levinson tied a tourniquet above Ishmael's right elbow, and then expertly tapped a vein in Ishmael's arm.

Dan watched the imam's blood filling the vial. Tears welled his eyes. He spoke slowly to Ishmael in English. "Jews have a name for what you are doing. *Mitzvah.* A good deed. We believe it brings God's blessings on you."

Ishmael stared back silently. He twisted his head until he caught the watchful eye of Al-Jabbar. Ever so carefully, he nodded at Rashid, elevated the three middle fingers of his left hand.

He drew his right thumb midway across the extended fingers and curled them until they disappeared in his fist.

~•∢

Before midnight, in the Lieutenant's hospital room …

Brother Byron re-entered, towing a night cleaning man with his broom still in hand. He gestured to the night assistant nurse and arranged his chosen witnesses at the foot of the bed.

"What are you up to?" Josh's voice was full of concern.

"Can you sit up for a marriage ceremony?"

Haja impulsively grasped the friar's hand. "Thank you, Thank you!"

"Mind you both, that this is not sacramental, but a civil ceremony."

"Fine. You really are a brother." Josh pressed his hand over Haja's, heartfelt gratitude in his voice.

"Your full name?" From his briefcase, the friar withdrew a wrinkled legal sheet of gold-embossed vellum paper and a pen.

"Joshua Isaacson."

"Isaacson." As he wrote, the friar glanced up. "Do you know why you're named Isaacson?"

Josh stared. "It's my father's name."

Byron resumed writing. "Age? Place of birth?"

"Twenty-one, born in Liberty Hill, South Carolina."

"Your full name?" Brother Byron turned to the girl.

"Haja Bin Kanaan." She began to cough nervously.

"K-a-n-a-a-n?"

Haja nodded.

The friar lifted his eyes from the paper. "Your first name is H-a-j-a?"

"Hagar at birth," her head shook. "After I was taken on the holy pilgrimage to Mecca, I was named again—Haja."

Brother Byron nodded, shaking his head slowly. "Age and place of birth?"

"Seventeen and ten months. Jericho, Palestine."

The friar's clear, graveled voice took on a practiced rhythm. "Do you swear before this licensed Civil Registrar, Brother Byron Nichols of Beirut, Lebanon, that the information you have given me is correct, and do you agree that if it is found false this certificate of marriage is not valid?"

"I do," Josh and Haja spoke in unison.

"I do solemnly declare that I know of no lawful reason why, I," the brother pointed at Josh, "say your first name, please."

"Joshua."

Brother Byron continued, "May not be joined in marriage to," he turned to Haja, "say your given name."

"Hagar."

"I now declare Joshua Isaacson and Hagar Bin Kanaan to be legally wedded husband and wife."

The nurse gave Haja flowers. The cleaning man shook Josh's hand.

"I call upon these persons here present to witness this ceremony in writing." Brother Byron extended pen and document to the hospital employees. "You will please sign here."

"That's it?" Josh was suddenly crestfallen.

"You can kiss your beautiful bride," Brother Byron grinned.

Josh slowly drew Haja's face into his hands with a pent-up, bashful tenderness, and bent her head to his. For his protection, Haja quickly turned her mouth away. Her hands caressed his wavy hair.

Tears streaming from her eyes, she looked directly at her husband. "Allahu Akbar."

Josh touched his yarmulke, bowed his head, and then gazed at his bride. "Baruch HaShem."

Fervently, they clasped each other's bodies.

Josh gasped for air. His hands went to a searing pain at his temple as he slumped backwards against the pillows.

part two

chapter ten

Seconds later, Tuesday, March 30 . . .

The assistant night nurse moved Haja's wheelchair aside, broke an ammonia capsule under the Lieutenant's nostrils, and pressed the crisis button above his bed. A silent blue light began to blink outside Josh's door and at the nurse station. Brother Byron quickly wheeled Haja into the corridor as technicians with resuscitation equipment rushed into the room and attempted to revive Josh.

Dr. Ramzy, awakened at home, gave instructions for the Intensive Care Unit's night duty physician to examine the lieutenant for signs of escalated hemorrhage, heart failure, and hypotension. As he hurried as fast as his arthritis allowed into his blue hospital scrubs for the car ride to the hospital, he reached Noor on her cell phone. He gave her instructions to have a medical helicopter fly immediately to the bloodmobile and airlift Lieutenant Isaacson's attending doctors and donor back to the hospital.

Minutes later, the hospital's chopper lifted off its brightly lit cement pad into the black Mediterranean mist.

The pilot commander made military code contact with the convoy's lead Humvee as it crawled on fog-bound Highway 4 and arranged a rendezvous within thirty minutes at the short, sandy airstrip east of Ashquelon in Israel.

By 5:45 a.m., as the orange sun peeped between the high-rises and over the roofs of Tel-Aviv-Yafo, Rose of Sharon doctors had stabilized Josh's breathing and pulse, and had administered two pints of cross-matched whole blood taken from Imam Ishmael Bin Kanaan.

The transfused blood boosted the lieutenant's platelet count, slowing the oozing, and signs of better coagulation became apparent around his wounds. He was started on triple antibiotics as preventive treatment to the possibility his hemorrhage was caused by the presence of infectious organisms in the blood. Josh's oxygen saturation improved, and his vitals started a swift return toward normal.

chapter eleven

Wednesday, March 31 late morning sunlight floods his room, Josh opens his eyes...

"You are out of danger, lieutenant..." Dr. Ramzy's stooped, tired body was supported by his canes. Smiling members of his emergency team surrounded him. "You had a traumatic twenty-four hours, but we've brought you back to normal. You have such a strong constitution. In no time, you'll be on your feet."

Josh stared into the glowing faces of his mother and father.

Dr. Ramzy went on. "You know, son, I have children of my own, but your dad gave me a lesson in what fatherhood truly means. At midnight last night he went into the treacherous streets of the Jabaliya camp. Along with Dr. Levinson and an IDF patrol, he brought back the donor whose blood helped purify your own, and is healing you now."

Applause filled the room. "It was a team effort!" Dr. Isaacson raised Dr. Levinson's arms. Both men, still dressed in surgery scrubs, grinned and waved.

Dr. Ramzy stepped aside. "The one we also want to thank is here," he pointed to the man coming through the door. "The person who gave his blood so that our young American should live. Imam bin Kanaan!"

Spontaneous applause rose up again as Ishmael was separated

from the custody of a hospital security guard standing with him. The imam wore a fresh purple jallabiya. A new black and white checkered kaffiyeh obscured most of his face wounds.

Dan Isaacson stepped forward, smiling. "When we encountered each other in Jabaliya, in the darkness and confusion, imam, you threw my medical bags away. But when you consented to give blood I said it was a mitzvah. Now, I have to admit to you ... " Dan stopped, emotion rising in his throat. Brushing at his eyes, he asked Noor to translate his English. He waited and then continued. "I have to confess, when I talked to your daughter, I did not recommend all I could have. In my mind there was an examination that could be done using a light anesthetic. I mentioned it to Dr. Ramzy. Dr. Richard Levinson agreed to assist me. You are her father. May I have your permission to do that procedure this afternoon?"

As Noor translated into Arabic, Ishmael's grey eyes grew impenetrable and he pretended not to understand. *Do I let this infidel American Jew touch Haja? If I say no, he can examine her anyway, and I become his enemy. If I say yes, he will see me as his friend and let me move about the hospital and finish our plan to destroy it.*

"Nurse, tell him," Dr. Isaacson wiped at his eyes, "that the same concern he showed for Joshua, I'm going to give for the life of his daughter. I already sent her blood sample to the States this morning."

Respectfully, Ishmael bowed his head. "Allahu Akbar."

"Baruch HaShem." Dan smiled earnestly.

Estee stepped toward to her son's bed. "Your nightmare is over. She stroked Josh's hand. "Dad asked the IDF to allow you to recuperate in South Carolina. They will let you go home this week, honey."

Both parents missed the stricken look in their son's eyes.

As a late morning light pierced the hospital's shadowy basement grilles...

Ishmael walked rapidly ahead of his guard along the corridor that circled the OR surgery bays. The imam nodded at the guard and slipped alone into the maintenance shop. Inside, on the floor, he saw containers with soap detergent labels near the door, and Rashid alone, shouting in Arabic on the phone. Ishmael locked the door behind him.

The engineer caught sight of his leader's purple robe, hung up instantly and grabbed a crowbar. Enraged, he leaped at him.

"Harm me ... " Ishmael moved away swiftly, and spoke quietly in their native tongue. "And your three daughters will be in peril."

"I'm going to kill you!"

"The community's is keeping them safe." Ishmael circled. "Safe from rash acts of yours like forcing me to give blood to an Israeli!" He touched the bruises on his face inflicted by the IDF soldiers and then flung out a hand at the boxes. "The mixture is here. You can start packing it into the chair!"

"You gave blood this morning under guard," Rashid stalked his imam. "How did you grab my girls?"

"The community took your girls from right under Salima's nose," Ishmael waved at the containers, "the same way your nitrate was delivered. Right under the Israelis' noses." He was bemused at the rage in his friend's face. "Calm yourself." He put his hands on the workbench.

Rashid raised the crowbar, and Ishmael jumped backwards. The bar crashed down on the wood.

"Now you threaten my life!" Ishmael kept moving. "But the other day you said all lives were holy to Allah. See how wrong you interpret Muhammad?"

"Give me my girls back!"

"You will get them back after you perform jihad."

Rashid's chest heaved. Gulping air with helpless desperation, he laid the crowbar on the bench, his burning eyes signaling surrender. "What do you want me to do?"

"Is the chair hollowed out?"

"Yes."

"Every section wired to the front wheel?" Ishmael saw Rashid nod wordlessly. "You load the chair tonight."

Rashid grabbed the folds of Ishmael's jallabiya. "Give my girls back to Salima and me. I am begging you. Without them, we have no reason to live!"

Ishmael removed himself from Rashid's desperate grip. "After you have performed your holy duty."

"Imam—Muhammad's first hadith," Rashid's voice broke into tortured cries, "Be good to your neighbor. I am your neighbor!"

"We are soldiers of the Qur'an, Rashid—"

The close friends breathed heavily, glaring at each other.

Rashid's mouth became a taunting grimace. "Two nights ago, here at Rose of Sharon … your daughter was married."

Ishmael's eyes blazed up. His long body shook.

"To an Israeli Army lieutenant in the hospital."

"May you rot in hell!" Ishmael leaped over a corner of the workbench, his hands aimed at Rashid's throat. "Liar!"

"Haja is now Joshua Isaacson's wife." Rashid folded his arms across his chest.

"The Americans!" Ishmael stopped in his tracks, shuddering. "Will they stop at nothing? First my blood and now my daughter!"

A faintly satisfied smile crossed Rashid's face as the imam fell to the ground and touched his forehead to the cement.

The entreating words of the *Fatihah*, the Qur'an's opening chapter, groaned from Ishmael's trembling lips. "In the name of Allah, the beneficent, the merciful, praise be to Allah, the lord of the worlds, the beneficent, the merciful, master of the day of requital. Thee do we serve and thee do we beseech for help … "

Ishmael's prayer trailed off into guilt and self-judgment. "I left her here alone. Was that my fault? I had to organize your mission." Freeing himself from guilt, he looked up sharply at the engineer. "Was it an Islamic or Jewish marriage?"

"Civil."

"Then it is not a death blow to our name. It is not marriage before Allah."

"Do you want to know what the cleaning worker told me?" Rashid offered. "At the ceremony he was best man."

The imam stiffened.

Rashid measured out the words. "'Before my very eyes,' he said, 'an unhappy, sick teenager blossomed into a happy, healthy and beautiful bride.'"

"I command you to prepare the wheelchair tonight," Ishmael's dark-blooded lips pursed into a grim line. "And have it ready by seven in the morning."

The engineer stared open-mouthed.

"We will do jihad to the hospital tomorrow," Ishmael intoned honorably. "Your friend, the American doctor and his son, are unholy, so they will die along with the others."

"You are going to kill the new bride and groom?"

"In the eyes of Allah there was no marriage."

"You have come a long way..." Rashid's voice was low and anguished, "From an innocent shepherd boy who loved his flock, to a schoolboy who played on the same basketball team with Christians and Hebrew boys, to an angry freedom fighter, to a holy preacher! And now you are a kidnapper of the children of your best friend! Tomorrow, you will be a mass murderer of the sick and the wounded and an executioner of two very blissful young people." He turned away. Tears fogged his eyes. "And I am your accomplice!"

Shaking off the words, Ishmael started for the door. "The wheelchair will be brought to you when the day shift ends. Work your community crew all night. One of them will return for it at six in the morning. Rashid..." The imam's head lifted, but his hawk's eyes held a touch of melancholy. "Rashid, in order to save the world, it is necessary to purify it."

◢━✦

In his room, the Lieutenant pushed away his emptied lunch tray...

"Mother?" Josh said.

Estee's heart sang. He had an appetite. His eyes were a sunny blue. The monitor screen registered a stable and normal pulse and temperature. *The new blood has saved my son.*

Josh stared at the gold-trimmed buttons on his mother's Ralph Lauren suit jacket. *So well dressed and so American. So far from the real world. I went away a teenager determined to keep terrorism from my folks, and crossed the barrier that keeps our world at war. How do I tell my mother I've fallen in love with a girl who lived all her life in a crowded, filthy refugee camp, with open sewage and no future, and for revenge, turned to terrorism?*

Estee grasped Josh's hand. "This war is going to be nothing but a bad dream for you. This weekend, you'll be recuperating on the upstairs porch and watching ships maneuver up Charleston Harbor. You'll have your flute, and your girlfriends. We'll get you a new radiophone so you and Junior can talk again to your Internet friends. All about your plans to find water and build new cities!"

"Mom, you're going to have to help me ... with Dad." Josh steeled his inner resolve. "I can't go back to South Carolina now."

"You've fought enough for the world. Your father wants you back home. So do I."

Josh inhaled. *I know these next words will throw her for a loop…just say it.* "Yesterday, Mom…last night…before my blood transfusion, Mother…I got married here. I'm a married man."

Estee's heartbeat faltered. "What? What—"

"She's a wonderful girl, Mom, all heart and mind. That singer I told you about. Her name is Haja."

I felt a premonition. Nausea flooded Estee's stomach. She clasped her abdomen to protect her fetus against his stabbing words. *How can he do this? Twenty-one years of nursing, raising, caring, and worrying over him. Haja!* Blood surged to her temples. "The Arab bomber who tried to kill Jews in Tel Aviv?" she managed. "The girl with a lung infection?"

"Dad said he'd do an endoscopy on her in the OR this afternoon. He has an idea." Josh's voice rose with hope.

"Suppose he confirms nothing can be done? How could you marry a girl so ill?" *A child who thinks he's a man. What a horrible mistake he has made. My God, the horrible disgrace to our faith, our community.*

"Mom, you told me, remember, that when you met Dad, love showed in the eyes right away? That he could have proposed marriage to you on the spot? When I first heard Haja sing, her voice took me right out of my agony. When I saw her for the first time, I felt as close to her as I do to anybody I've ever known, even to you. And when she saw me, the same feelings overcame her. Mom, I can't fly off and leave her. Will you tell Dad?"

Dazed, Estee rose. "Your battalion phoned and said your

sick leave can begin right away. We'll all fly to the States tomorrow and have your marriage annulled there."

"Mother, no!"

Estee walked on uncertain feet. "No? Then you tell your father his firstborn married an Arab ... who murders Jews. Put an ax in his heart yourself."

"Mother, no!"

Josh spoke to an empty doorway.

Rose of Sharon's Security Ward, noon; inside the floral curtains about Haja's corner bed ...

"Situ!" The bowed eighty-seven year-old peasant wrapped in a shapeless lilac chador from sandals to her white hair shook Haja's bed insistently, whispering in Arabic. "Situ—"

Haja's eyes opened, unfocused.

"Child." The bent figure repeated the family's traditional greeting used to address all family members, "Situ ... "

Slowly rising from her pillow, Haja blinked, staring into the kind, withered face framed by the dark shawl. "Grandma! I am dreaming—" she said in Arabic.

"My eyes see you one more time! Thank'ess Allah!" Situ bin Kanaan, widowed matriarch of a Palestine dynasty, clasped the only young person left from her happy, pastoral family. She held Haja to her bosom, crooning in shaky, husky tones, "Long time no see, Situ sweetheart, my sweetheart!"

"I am dreaming of you. Oh, Grandma! Grandma!"

"I want to roll stuffed grape leaves for you, chop mint for

tabboulleh." Situ held up shaking hands. "Fingers strong no more."

"You have cooked meals for a lifetime, grandma!" Without warning, words from her dream tumbled from Haja's lips. "I have found my man, Situ! I must do shaheda! I have found my man and I must do shaheda!"

Softly, Situ wiped at the tears coursing down the youthful face cradled in her arms.

"Why is my life so hard? Why is Papa so cruel?" Haja sobbed, helplessly.

"My sweetheart … " Situ cried with her grandchild.

The floral track curtains parted around the bed. "I told you to wait downstairs for me." Ishmael strode inside, scolding his mother in Arabic. "Mama, you promised to do what I tell you here." Magnetic in his flowing jallabiya, his checkered kaffiyeh partly shielded his swollen face.

"Abouya!" Haja looked up at the towering imam, continuing in Arabic. "How is he? Noor told me you gave blood." She straightened, coughing.

Ishmael planted himself in front of his mother. "I have scheduled jihad," he murmured.

"How is he?"

"Who?"

"The Lieutenant?"

A tremor coursed through Ishmael. He swallowed the choking fury he felt at the American's mere name. Since leaving Rashid earlier in the day, he had convinced himself that jihad and Haja's volunteer role as a shaheda overshadowed the shame she had brought his name. As she had matured quickly in childhood, he had treated her more as an adult and as someone he depended on, much as he had depended on his wife. All alone now, his trust had snapped, and so he replied flatly. "The Lieutenant's doctor-father will make an examination of you today. I had no choice but to give my permission."

"Father, how is the Lieutenant?" Haja addressed him, formally.

"The Jew will recover. Later this week his father tries to take him to the United States."

"To America?" Haja's velveteen voice cracked.

Ishmael walked to the wheelchair standing near the window and moved it toward the bed. "But he will not escape. Nor will his father."

He screened himself to block off his mother again. His voice turned softly incisive and inspired. "Community members are writing a great speech now. You will read it. You will reject peace with Israel. You will urge total resistance. You will demand the right of Arabs to return and to regain the land seized from us."

"Father—?"

"I have watched you practice on the roof with this," Ishmael's earth-hardened hand touched the wheelchair. "This afternoon, go up once more. Practice for the last time. Remember, the left front wheel must hit the metal base of a light pole to trigger the charge." His voice dropped further. "Jihad is—"

"Father?" Haja interjected.

"Jihad is tomorrow morning."

"Abouya?" Haja raised her hand for permission to speak.

Ishmael permitted no interruptions. "Your chair will be prepared tonight and brought here near sunrise. Later in the morning, one of us will take you up to the roof and make your video. Then, count fifteen minutes on your watch. Then take aim, a long run, and crash your chair into a pole." Ishmael's eyes brimmed, but he hardened his lips. "In the blink of an eyelash, you will be in a place of honor in paradise!"

Situ hobbled a few steps forward, her frail figure even with Ishmael. "Situ—"

"Mama, go outside and wait for me."

Situ quickly struck away her son's restraining arm, taking a deep breath. "Situs, my children. I don't hear you both good." She threw up her hands. "I just see your faces and eyes." She peered at them, struggling with the seething thoughts in her mind. "Yasir, my oldest son gone, Tamir gone, Usama, your mama Mariyah, and your sisters, gone. Mister bin Kanaan in heaven. All gone from our farm because of war … Ishmael now an imam of war—"

"Mama, you think from the heart, not the head." Ishmael grasped his mother's sleeve.

"'Oo, 'scuse me, I never learn to read, I know." Situ glanced from Haja up to Ishmael, fear and foreboding filling her eyes. "Always, Kanaans never lock doors to anyone, are family of peace. Daddy and I live in—"

"Situ, no time for this." Ishmael interrupted, turning his mother toward the curtains. "You go to the waiting room at the end of the hall. You wait there for me, Mama." Firmly, he led her out.

Within a moment, he was back. "My daughter, by tomorrow, your video will be given to *Al Jazeera* and you will become a beloved martyr around the world."

Haja's mouth trembled. "I don't want to die. I can't do shahada."

"Jihad is set."

"I have only days to live, the doctors told me. I want to live every one I can—"

Ishmael's fingers rose for silence. "Repeat after me. Dying as a martyr does not mean real death!"

Haja's mouth tightened.

"You have always been obedient to your father's commands—always. Do as the Qur'an has ordered. Repeat. 'Dying as a martyr does not mean real death.'"

Haja's face paled.

"Did you not say the way to stop bullets was to become a bomb? Repeat what I said." Ishmael's eyes glowed with emotion. "Repeat what I said!"

Haja pursed her lips closer.

Ishmael bent on one knee, beside the bed. His voice quivered. "Just as our first father, Ibrahim, offered Ishmael on the altar to show obedience, so I now offer the lamb closest to my chest into your great arms."

Haja stared at her father as he prayed. Filial obedience coursed in her. Her courage to defy him faltered. She turned her head away.

"Repeat!" Ishmael, bent in prayer, demanded.

"Dying as a martyr doesn't mean real death," Haja whispered.

"Praise to Allah." With a happy, proud smile, Ishmael rose to his feet.

Nurse Noor entered through the curtains admitting an excited Dr. Levinson, accompanied by Dan Isaacson.

"Dr. Isaacson and I have been busy arranging for your test," Dr. Levinson announced to her in English. Haja, your father has granted his permission." He nodded his head at Ishmael. "Have you informed your daughter, sir?"

"Allahu Akbar." Ishmael inclined his kaffiyeh slightly, stealing a knowing sidewise glance at Haja.

Dan Isaacson held up a slender, elegant instrument. "Young lady, this device is an endoscope. It has lenses and a light source that will allow us to study your bronchial tubes. That may provide additional clues about your illness and its treatment. We will first give you a slight anesthetic so you will not feel any discomfort at all."

Dr. Levinson grasped the pearl wheelchair. "Now, we're going to take you down to surgery."

Noor helped Haja sit in the chair. The doctors moved ahead. Behind them, Ishmael cautioned Noor in Arabic. "I command you—do not leave my daughter alone with any man. Return her right here to me!"

Haja sat upright as she was wheeled away, frantically pleading with Noor to take her to her husband.

Forty-five minutes later, in the basement corridor…

Noor pushed Haja's chair out of the OR toward the elevators. Haja opened her eyes in time to see Noor's fingers poised at the third floor button.

"You promised." She whispered in Arabic.

"Your father's waiting in the security ward," Noor licked her lips nervously.

"You must take me to Joshua's room."

"Your father is—"

"Please, nurse," Haja inhaled sadly. "All of our lives are but candles in the wind—".

Stopped by the fatalistic words, Noor stared into Haja's haunted eyes and silently pressed the higher button.

The elevator door slid back on the fourth floor. Noor quickly moved Haja down the hall. She reached the Lieutenant's room and whispered hotly, "I must go in with you. I promised your father not to let you out of my sight."

Haja wheeled herself inside. Noor swung the door closed behind them. Haja stopped the chair and looked lovingly at Josh.

Upon seeing her, he sat up. His face broke into an astonished smile. Throwing off his covers, he swung his feet on the floor and rushed toward her.

Haja climbed from her chair and embraced him.

Josh buried her face against his shoulder. "What did the endoscopy show? How are you?"

"There is some chance for me! I heard your father say it!"

"How I prayed for you!" Josh choked.

"And you? Is it all right for you to be up?" Her hands caressed him.

"I'm his number one physical specimen, Dr. Ramzy says. I'm on the road to recovery." He grinned. "Happy anniversary, wife, we are two days old!"

"Oh, Joshua!" She looked into his eyes, the slight blush in her cheeks draining ash-white. "There is terrible news—"

A knock sounded at the door. Haja ducked behind Josh. Noor edged open the door. Rashid stood there with Brother Bryan. He quickly moved the robed friar ahead of him into the room and closed the door.

"Congratulations to you, Lieutenant." Rashid spoke rapidly in English. His agonized black eyes spotted Haja. "I heard you speak English. Congratulations to you, Haja. I am Rashid Ibn Habas, head of the maintenance department. Do you remember me from Jericho? I repaired machinery on your grandfather's farm? I have confided to Brother Byron my activities with your father. All of them!"

Haja moved beside Josh, staring into Rashid's caramel-colored face. Despite his moustache and his half-glasses, she recognized her father's childhood friend.

"Lieutenant..." Brother Byron stepped toward Josh, speaking in his clipped Scottish manner, "Rashid came to advise me there is a plot to destroy Rose of Sharon. The plan is to pack a wheelchair with explosives and detonate it tomorrow, using a suicide bomber."

Noor gasped in horror. Josh's face emptied of color. "My parents," he spoke numbly, "planned to take me to the States tomorrow. They got me an Army sick leave. But I told my mother I'd stay in the hospital."

"Imam Ishmael … " Rashid spoke with tortured effort, "has kidnapped three of my daughters. Only after the hospital is bombed will he release them."

Brother Byron turned to Haja. "Does your father know you and the Lieutenant are married?"

"I told him early this morning," Rashid nodded his head. "I begged him to cancel the mission."

"Tomorrow morning," Haja spoke slowly, "my father commanded me to be the suicide bomber."

Noor stepped back. Her hand's hands flew to her mouth in terrified disbelief.

"He asked you to sit in the chair and destroy yourself, your husband, and so many of us?" Brother Byron added, gently, "You could not say no to him?"

"I … I've never in my life said no to him." Haja's eyes held an anguished plea for Josh and the others. "Israeli soldiers killed his father … and a sister of Rashid before his eyes. All his brothers and his sister … even my mother and the children, ran away to other countries. Only he stayed to fight for our land. I stayed with him."

Tears filled her eyes, and her voice wavered, "I wanted to give my life to make him smile at me again. This morning," she clasped Josh's hands, "I could not say no to my father, even if your love gave me the courage to be your wife … even if I am to die."

"He is in the security ward waiting for her. He could be on

his way here now." Noor's voice quavered. "We must report all this to Dr. Ramzy. He'll alert security." She moved to the door.

Rashid's cautionary hand stopped her. "We have people in security. Others beside me will strike quickly. There will be much bloodshed." He grimaced in shame. "Community members—secret members—are everywhere in the hospital. Brother Byron has a plan to stop the operation. It can also save Sharon's patients and personnel, and my daughters."

"What is the plan?" Josh looked trustfully at the friar, "Tell us?"

Silently, Brother Byron glided to the door and locked it. *I have a plan all right. But its chances for success are filled with peril. If it fails it can inflame the Mideast. Did it come to me because cancer has the best of me? No, it came because of the courage of these two youngsters.*

"The plan came to me as a bolt from the sky." The brother looked from the newlyweds to Noor and Rashid. "I am a Franciscan, and we live by bolts from the heavenly world. But if we follow them in this world, they can lead to dangerous actions and consequences, even as mortals call it, to death. This plan calls for great daring and courage. Each one of you must give your own answer to this question—are you ready to leave the hospital with me tonight?"

"They can't. They are too weak!" Noor cried.

"If they stay," Byron said, flatly, "they will be separated by their families, blown up by a bomb, or murdered. That last part includes the rest of the hospital, as well as Rashid and his daughters. My plan will stop the bombing before it can start.

If you agree, Nurse Noor, will you care for Lieutenant and Mrs. Isaacson?"

"Where will you take them?"

"So no one can let any information slip, I'd best not tell." Brother Byron was serene.

"Our love gives us more strength, Nurse," Haja whispered. "Give our love a chance."

"And you, Rashid," Brother Byron turned to the engineer, "will you come?"

"I am for the people of Palestine—," Rashid brimmed with passion. He swallowed. "But there is a hadith about a messenger who came to the Prophet and asked, 'what do you think about a person who loves a people but leaves them?' Muhammad answered. 'Each is with those he loves.' As a boy," the engineer lowered his eyes, "I fashioned slings for my people to throw rocks. As a man, I designed bombs for my people to detonate. The more enemies I destroyed by day," his head came up, a tremor choked his voice, "the more tortured Allah's love in my heart became at night. Love is all I live for! For my four daughters. For my wife, and their future. And now, for Haja and her American. The Prophet Muhammed says in Hadith eighteen, 'follow up your wrongdoing with a good deed that shall erase it.' I'll go with you."

Josh smiled at Rashid. He turned to the friar. "Brother Byron, why will you risk your life for two strangers?"

"Life in the Mideast is a catch-twenty-two life." The Brother's keen eyes pierced the couple. "Hatred masquerades as heroism. War masquerades as peace. You two break the cycle."

He grasped Haja's wheelchair. "Rashid, these are the drilled out arms and wheels you were ordered to pack with explosives tonight?"

Rashid nodded. "The entire chair has to be packed—except for one battery to run on."

"As you work, will you be watched?"

"By the Imam's community mujahid leader, a paramedic here. What Ishmael orders, Al-Jabbar executes. He rode in the bloodmobile Wednesday night to find Ishmael in Gaza. He read the specs for the wheelchair."

"Can you disable the chair without his notice? Install some mechanism to make it safe and unable to explode?"

The engineer squatted beside the chair. He narrowed his eyes, willing his mind to go into the circuitry. He moved his fingers on the undercarriage, musing out loud. "The wire from the battery box goes in this tube…the tube connects to this rod in the wheel…when the rod strikes metal the explosives are detonated." He thought a moment. "I can short the pressure plate that releases the rod. That will disable the bombing device."

Brother Byron grinned his approval. "What time will the Imam's followers leave you?"

"Midnight."

"Will they take the chair?"

"No. When the day shift starts, someone will call for it."

"Then, at two this morning, can you secretly wheel it to the rear of the Tomb of the Patriarchs replica—the padlocked building in the hospital courtyard?"

"Why there?"

"It is never guarded. I have a key. We can assemble there safely. It has a sunken roadway out of the hospital grounds." Byron pointed to Noor. "To all this, Nurse, what do you say? Will you join us?"

A picture of Jordan's Queen Mother flashed in Noor's mind. "Working for freedom means choices and risks." Nervously, she wet her lips. "What must I do?"

"Your job," Brother Byron explained, "will be to bring adequate medical supplies, including sedatives just in case— and…Lieutenant and Mrs. Isaacson also, to the same place at the Patriarch's building, just after midnight."

A tremulous, defiant laugh escaped the nurse's slender throat. "You can count on Noor."

⤙⤚

Within the maintenance shop as Sharon's eleven o'clock chimes sounded…

Al-Jabbar, from his position as the guard inside the darkened workroom, shined his high beam flashlight just ahead of Rashid and the second mujahid. The light illuminated a path toward the rear of the workshop. All three men wore safety glasses, facemasks, and triple sets of yellow elbow length latex gloves. Inching along ever so carefully to protect against deadly splatters, Rashid and the second helper carried the footrest filled with nitrate mix and fuel oil from the workbench to the pearl wheelchair. Slowly, they lowered it into its base position.

Raising his head, Rashid turned his pocket flashlight back at his bench, past the almost depleted bags of RDX powder, fertilizer, tools, and scales, to the only dismantled chair parts remaining to be packed, the three remaining small wheels. *Now!* he thought. *Order Ishmael's paramedic and the helper to fill them. That will keep them occupied while I work on the left front caster. I must be precise and quick. Al-Jabbar, Ishmael's second in command, is watching me like a hawk. I'll give him a job to do.*

Using his flashlight, he motioned the paramedic and his helper to the bench, signaling instructions with his hands and pointing at the right front wheel. After the men had poured the explosives into the caster, he took it cautiously and carried it to the rear. Hiding his movements at the chair with his body, he secured it in position. In a lightning move, he switched his hands to the left front wheel, coughed to cover a muffled noise from his clippers, worked for a few scant seconds more, and straightened up.

Ten minutes later, the deadly chair stood completely reassembled, appearing as innocently functional as before. Rashid cleared his bench while the helper straightened the room and Al-Jabbar swept the floor.

A glint of aluminum caught Al-Jabbar's eye. He bent down and picked up a short piece of tubing. *It stinks from dung and gunpowder. It's wet and warm... could this come from the wheelchair? It's been clipped off. Without it, will the chair explode?*

The paramedic slid the tube into his green coveralls and kept sweeping.

The men finished their work and then removed and stowed their protective gear. Outside, the three of them went separate ways in the deserted corridors.

The hospital's chimes began to strike midnight.

chapter twelve

Thursday, April Fools Day, minutes after midnight in Rose of Sharon's basement...

Al-Jabbar moved quietly back along the empty corridor to the maintenance door, opened it with one of his passkeys, and slipped back inside the shop, now lit only by a rear wall night-light. He stood still for a moment, making sure the room was deserted, and then tiptoed to the pearl wheelchair. From his coverall pockets he took out the piece of short tubing, a pen flashlight, and a schematic of the chair wiring. He bent to his knees and clasped his hands in silent prayer. Then, he twisted his flashlight and methodically inspected the chair. When he reached the undercarriage, he saw the tubing from the battery box to the wheel was disconnected. With extreme care, he reconnected the wiring to the pressure plate and spliced the piece of connecting tubing securely back in place.

⌁

In the 4.a.m. blackness behind the Tomb of the Patriarchs replica building...

Shadowy figures boarded a darkened Sharon medical van. Another figure opened the rear metal door and lifted a wheelchair inside. The vehicle crept up the rear ramp of the building and made its way out of the grounds, onto the Tel Aviv-Yafo streets, where it turned on the Ayalan River road and continued out of the city, to the southeast.

⌒⥝

As the medical van drove the Tel Aviv-Jerusalem freeway...

Cutting through the dark Mediterranean coastal plain, the hospital van passed boldly lit airplane factories, stretches of white sand dunes, and moonlit grain and fruit orchards. Due to its black-on-white government license plates, it was waved through three checkpoints and it sped up and down Judean rolling hills dotted with wild flower clusters and encampments of Bedouin desert tribes. Josh, in Army clothes, and Haja in her hospital greens, slept wrapped in warm blankets on two suspended wall cots, with their hands joined. Noor sat beside them bundled in a dark coat over her white hospital uniform. In the rear, amidst bottles of oxygen, boxes of supplies, Rashid dozed in the swaying pearl wheelchair.

⌒⥝

Near Highway 38, in the glow of the van's dashboard lights...

"You are twenty-four hours from your blood transfusion." As he turned left onto a new road, Brother Byron spoke to the lieutenant who had climbed onto the front seat next to him. "How do you feel?"

"Dr. Ramzy's number one patient is getting stronger and stronger." Josh smiled, comforted by the friar's Scot accent.

"That's all the new Arab blood in you." Byron grinned.

"I've been thinking about that," Josh laughed. "Where are we headed?"

"Due south."

"To where?"

"Where the stakes are much higher than in Tel Aviv." Byron's green eyes remained fixed on the rough road. "Where every move we make will be dangerous and will be reported around the world."

"I always placed my life in the hands of Jewish rabbis before." Josh peered into the black pre-dawn. "You Brothers are Catholics, aren't you? Now, my wife and I are in the hands of a follower of Jesus."

Brother Byron laughed. "Wasn't he a Jewish rabbi?"

<hr>

Six a.m., Tel Aviv-Yafo, in the Rose of Sharon basement…

Al-Jabbar knocked softly on the maintenance department door, waited, and then rapped again. Finally, he used his pass-key. The shop confronted him, exactly as it looked at midnight, workbench and floor swept clear of fertilizer and fuel. *Where's Rashid, the engineer, the guy I suspect tried to cripple the chair last night? My orders are to pick it up from him here and deliver it first thing to the dispatch room. Nobody's here.* The slender paramedic searched the back of the shop. *Where's the chair? It's gone!*

In panic, Al-Jabbar quit the room and rushed into the hallway. It was crowded with drowsy workers punching their morning time cards. In his commonplace employee coveralls, he threaded his way to the back exit stairs, double timed up to the third floor, and hurried to the security ward.

Waving his ID badge at the soldier guarding the green doors, he trotted past sleeping patients to the end of the ward, and stuck his head between the curtains that surrounded Haja bin Kanaan's bed. The girl was asleep under the covers. Her wheelchair was nowhere in sight. *Where is it? Who has it? In Allah's name, where's the chair, where's Rashid?*

The paramedic scurried out of the ward and walked quickly down the corridor. He came to the conference room. Through its picture window, he saw his leader, Imam bin Kanaan, standing with Dr. Ramzy, more hospital bosses, and a well-dressed, bareheaded American-looking woman who wore her hair long. Next to her, at the blackboard, was a white-coated doctor with a prayer hat on his curls and evil blue eyes. *That's the Jew who forced blood from my imam in the bloodmobile. In just a few hours, the Americans will get their just reward!*

Inside the crowded conference area, Ishmael crinkled his forehead, trying to understand Dr. Isaacson's English words.

"South Carolina received this patient's endoscopic biopsy slide late yesterday. My residents spent the night on the Internet comparing slides from cases in pathology journals. They believe the patient suffers from glucan pnuemonitis, lung inflammation caused by inhalation of a massive amount of finely ground grain fibers." Dan Isaacson paused for an intern to translate his words into Hebrew and Arabic. "The beta-glucan was somehow micro-pulverized and aerosolized to make dangerous inflammatory lung poison resulting in slow death."

Dan faced Ishmael, addressing him with a mixture of emotions—fatherly disbelief, a parent's horror, and yet humble warmth for his son's savior. "When your daughter breathed the fumes from that homemade bomb in her backpack—it poisoned her lungs. Explosives combined in a wrong way were the cause, possibly. Haja's white cells have attacked her lungs, causing her to drown in her own secretions, now."

Ishmael narrowed his eyes in an attempt to deny the doctor's words. He drew himself up to his full, ascetic height. *So the smart American Hebe found out it was the vapors from the bran I used. It could have been bad when I purchased it in Cairo. It could have turned bad when we mixed it in Jabiliya with the explosives that went into the backpack. Then, when she began to board that Tel Aviv bus and the bomb leaked, it caused her sickness. It's too late for these stupid doctors to do anything, anyway, because in two hours they—*

Ishmael felt some round green pills being pressed in his hands.

"Would you like to cure your daughter?" Dan Isaacson was smiling.

Ishmael peered into the doctor's happy eyes. The unexpected question hit a hidden nerve.

"Have her take one every morning with lots of fluids. They're Cytoxan, and should reduce or stop the inflammatory response. That, along with watchful respiratory and nursing care should help her improve. C'mon, let's go down the hall and give her the first pill!"

Dr. Ramzy and Estee Isaacson congratulated him in different languages. Suppressing his mixed feelings, Ishmael forced a smile onto his bewildered, troubled face. A band of joyous hospital staffers moved with him out the door and toward the security ward. As the news spread along the hallway, passing personnel broke into spontaneous applause. Al-Jabbar trailed the group.

The paramedic slowed halfway through the ward because of the jam of people in front of him. He heard cries of worry and dismay as several doctors, nurses, and aides threaded through the crowd. He wormed to the corner window close to Imam Ishmael and realized the truth. Haja's curtains were thrown back and there was no sign of the patient. Words flew around his ears in languages he couldn't follow.

"Quiet, please! One at a time!" Dr. Ramzy' baritone boomed, first in Hebrew and then in English.

"When I came to work I saw her asleep in bed," a nurse declared in Hebrew.

"You saw this!" Shouting in Arabic, a cleaning worker held up towels curled under a black scarf to resemble a dark head.

"The Lieutenant's flown his coop!" In disheveled green scrubs, fourth floor nurse Carol Ann Tarcai burst forward into Dr. Ramzy's view, mixing Irish accented English and Hebrew. "Lieutenant Isaacson's flown his coop!" As the Chief Surgeon raised a bewildered eyebrow, Josh's nurse shouted hysterically, "His uniform has flown, too!"

"What does she mean?" Estee Isaacson's voice rose shrilly.

"Nurse Tarcai! Carol Ann!" Dr. Ramzy shook the woman's sturdy arms.

"Tarcai means Lieutenant Isaacson is gone," an English-speaking medic explained.

"My son gone?" Dan Isaacson turned to him.

"Where?" Dr. Ramzy waggled his cane helplessly. "Where's my assistant? Where is Noor?"

"She's not in this morning," a volunteer aide replied.

"Where has my son gone?" Dan Isaacson repeated.

Estee clutched her husband's arm, panicked that the horrible secret was out. "Haja and Joshua went away together. Perhaps…"

"What are you talking about? Why would they be together?" Confused, Dan frowned at his wife. "Why would they even be together? Why?"

Involuntarily, Estee's hands curled around her abdomen. Trembling, crying, she met her husband's eyes. "They are married! They married Tuesday night!"

Dan stared at his wife, and grasped at the wall as if he had been shot. His face was white. "What are you talking about? Tuesday?" Flushing, his voice rose. "You let it happen? You tell me Thursday?" He whirled to Carol Ann Tarcai. "You both let it happen? Why didn't anyone inform me?" He was suddenly aware that nurses and doctors of differing identities were witnessing his anguish. "This is a tragedy!" he choked out. "For generations, we are an orthodox Jewish family!"

Al-Jabbar took advantage of an embarrassed silence to whisper into Ishmael's ear the news of the missing wheelchair, and the missing engineer, Rashid.

Captain Ariel Cohen, Sharon's Security Chief, shouldered

his way to Dr. Ramzy's side, speaking English in a confidential voice. "One of our bloodmobiles was stolen from the hospital last night." He displayed a police teletype report. "The two of them must have run away in it. It's been located this morning across the country. In Hebron."

"Hebron?" Rafael Ramzy's voice spiked.

"Outside the Tomb of the Patriarchs."

"The real Tomb of the Patriarchs?" Dr. Ramzy's head jerked up painfully. "Why in God's name would they go there?"

"I'm going after them right now!" Captain Cohen's grim tone was icy.

"You must take me with you." Dan Isaacson stepped forward.

"We have to protect our son." Estee Isaacson moved beside her husband.

"I protect my daughter!" Ishmael pushed close to the Americans, his face in torment.

Ishmael's anguish moved Carol Ann Tarcai to push her way alongside the imam. "Haja and the Lieutenant need a nurse's care. I'll be the volunteer."

Captain Cohen cinched his web belt of weapons below his barrel chest. "I've picked an experienced squad of soldiers. That place is an international time bomb waiting to go off."

"How long will it take you to get us to Hebron?" Dr. Ramzy asked.

"Within the hour, Doctor." The Captain added, "By helicopter gunship."

Dr. Ramzy glanced at the agitated faces of the parents in

front of him. "Each of us has a personal interest." His solemn eyes glowing, he hobbled from the ward on his canes. "I'll lead the way."

～

Below the helicoptor's whirring blades, Thursday morning traffic snaked through Tel Aviv and Jaffa…

With unseeing eyes, Dr. Rafael Ramzy stared through the front window of the CH-53E panther helicopter as it powered off the hospital's helicopter circle. Beneath the camouflaged ship, cars and trucks shrank in size as they moved quickly on tree-lined boulevards and cobble-stoned alleys. At five hundred feet, the IDF pilot banked the crouching American-made gunship through clear blue skies and headed eastward over Highway 1.

Today is April Fools Day. Thoughts of the day and his father crowded out everything else in Rafael's mind. *Ten years ago today, the Patriarchs building Dad replicated on Sharon's compound closed. Why did the Isaacson boy and his bride run off to Hebron on April first? Coincidence? Hidden meaning? Why would they go to Hebron where barely five hundred Jewish settlers and one hundred fifty thousand Palestinians live? Year after year, fanatical Jews and Arabs challenge each other and shed blood in Hebron. Every major religion in the world stations officials there to report the grim statistics. Then a black eye for the Middle East and its peoples is trumpeted to the world. And we who struggle for a better life descend deeper into humiliation and hopeless despair.* Abruptly, Rafael saw Ammon Ramzy's reflection in the helicopter windshield—the hope filled black eyes in his father's noble face. A memory occurred to him—the white-haired surgeon walking at night with his eyes cocked toward distant Mount Zion in a confident, faithful search for the first evening star.

The doctor shook the image from his head. *Danger lies ahead, Dad, real danger.*

From his seat next to his wife in the second row in his white medical jacket, Dan Isaacson leaned toward an exit door jump seat where Sharon's Security Chief Captain Cohen sat with Dr. Levinson, the hospital's blood bank director. Both men wore radio earphones. The laptop computers on their knees were open. "When we land at the airport," Dr. Isaacson asked uneasily in English, "what's our plan to get Josh to safety?"

"We are at work on it now," Captain Cohen answered in English, looking up from a map of Hebron's mountain and valley roads. "When we land, we work under the PA, the Palestinian Authority. We are in contact with them now." He touched his earphones. The Police Commander of the West Bank is flying to meet us at the airport."

"Is he an Arab?" Estee Isaacson's face creased with further worry.

"Yes, Ma'm," Captain Cohen nodded.

From the third row seat alongside Al-Jabbar and Nurse Tarcai, Ishmael spoke loudly in English. "First, we must secure the safety of my daughter. Haja is only a child."

"A child?" Estee Isaacson called out. "Every child knows Arabs control Hebron. His daughter has led our son to the Philistines!"

"You are the Philistines!" Ishmael's tormented voice rose. "You came to our country and stole our land."

"Abraham the prophet paid for this land!" Estee snapped.

"Cover your head, female! Go back to godless America!"

"You must not fight," pleaded Nurse Carol Ann. "Both of your children are in danger—"

"Go back to other Arab countries." Estee stood up. "God gave this land to the Jews!"

Ishmael rose from his seat. "This is Arab land!"

"Read the Old Testament, you fool!" Estee shouted.

Dan Isaacson sprang up in front of his wife.

"From the beginning we are here." Shaking, Ishmael raised both arms at the Isaacsons. "We will be here forever!"

Whipping off seatbelts, IDF soldiers thrust rifles between the quarrelers.

⌒⌣

On a wall bench inside a darkened building in Hebron…

"Dear husband, how do you feel?" Haja snuggled against Josh's uniform.

"Getting stronger and stronger," Josh smiled. "That's what I told Brother Byron while you were asleep."

Opening her eyes to the gloom, Haja inhaled. "What time is it?"

"It's morning."

"I want to wake up this way every morning." She listened to the echo of her English words. "We are away from the sea?"

"We've climbed three thousand feet higher than the Mediterranean Sea. If the air's too thin for you, use the green oxygen concentrator. Noor strapped two portable units around our waists." Josh touched hers. "They're easy to use. And we're safe here. Brother Byron drove us to Hebron. We're in the Tomb of the Patriarchs."

"Ya Elahy!" Haja sat up quickly. Her eyes swept through the empty sanctuary, with its unlit golden chandeliers above layers of Arabian carpets below. "Oh my God," she repeated in English. Her voice fell to a whisper. "Joshua, next to Mecca, this is one of our holiest mosques."

"Next to the Jerusalem wall, in Jewish history, this is our holiest temple."

"Ibrahim, the father of the Muslims, is buried here." Haja went on. She stood up, fearful. "Bringing us here will bring us great trouble."

"Brother Byron must know what he's doing. He's coming right back. Noor's off exploring." Josh glanced upwards at the huge green-glowing limestone walls beautified with ancient sculptures and ancient tapestries. Forty feet above their heads, he glimpsed an emerald marble cupola topped by a gold ceiling skylight that filtered in dim daylight. "This castle was built three thousand years ago in the time of King Solomon!" His voice spilled hushed wonder. "About eight centuries before that, this whole place was an empty field. The Old Testament writers identified it as *Machpelah*. Abraham bought it for four hundred silver coins from a Canaanite."

"A Canaaanite?" Haja smiled. "That's me!"

"On our marriage certificate you spelled it with a K," Josh grinned.

"English or Arabic, it's the same name. Who was Abraham? Why did he buy it?"

"He was the father of all the Jews, and purchased it to bury his family. See that?" Josh pointed to an ornate mausoleum that stood off to itself on the carpet. Richly striped in red and gold, with a closed black roof, it stood fifteen feet high and was surrounded by a protective metal railing. "That's Isaac's tomb. There are supposed to be six tombs here. For Sarah, Abraham, his son Isaac, his grandson Jacob, and their wives … and maybe one for the first man God created, Adam."

Josh's voice dipped to a whisper. "But inside they're empty. *Machpelah* in Hebrew means a double cave. In the cave below, it's said, the bodies are buried … "

Haja gazed around the still, majestic edifice, drawing a deep breath and listening to the silence. Involuntarily, she shuddered, "The souls here cry out to speak!"

Josh put his arms around her. "The dead can't harm us."

Noor rushed nervously into sight across the thick carpets from the main doors. "People must be outside! I hear voices!"

A shaft of morning sun shone on the carpets and revealed Brother Byron in his brown robe and sandals, pushing Haja's pearl wheelchair. It was loaded with provisions. Some twenty people followed him, arms full of duffel bags, toolboxes, and sound equipment. Quickly, Rashid bolted the doors behind them. The Brother crossed the red carpets to Josh, Haja, and Noor.

"Meet all your friends—your committee of witnesses." Calmly introducing them by group, Brother Byron spoke in English. "The three in brown habits are Franciscan brothers.

They care for Roman Catholic interests in Palestine. So do these two nuns in grey robes with their faces veiled. They're members of the Poor Clares of Assisi. The civilians wearing safe-conduct vests keep their eyes on Israeli-Palestine clashes in Hebron. All of them have lost their patience with the violence and suffering; they report to their headquarters." Brother Byron smiled. "They have agreed to be witnesses to your marriage."

"Isn't this place under the PA? How did you get us and all of them past Arab guards?" Josh asked, astounded.

"We have our friends." Brother Byron grinned, "The presence of these observers will give pause to our pursuers who just landed here at the airport."

"Pursuers?" Haja didn't understand.

"Two helicopters just arrived. Hospital security, IDF soldiers, your father, the lieutenant's parents, and whatever Palestinian Authority forces will join their visit to us."

Brother Byron took a deep breath. "Now—our plan goes into effect. When they open these doors, the visitors will see this in front of their very eyes." He put his hand on the wheelchair. "Some of them will believe this is a bomb ready to explode the mosque and do away with everyone in an instant. That will stop them in their tracks. That will give us time to talk to them before your witnesses—the eyes and ears of the world." His eyes swung to Noor. "Will you please lay out your medical supplies?" Noor nodded, following him as he back-tracked across the mosque, issuing directions to the witnesses.

Josh and Haja watched the newcomers unravel red extension cords and string wires, start a power generator, switch on lights, set up recording equipment and cameras, place Haja's empty wheelchair in front of the main door, and plant sound speakers in two bushy trees outside the mosque entrance.

Haja drew Josh close. "When they see the disrespect to this holy mosque, the Arabs and my father will be inflamed with anger. If this is Abraham's burial hall, so will the Jews, and your father, too." Hard, lonely tears formed in her eyes. "I am the cause of all this trouble. Because I love you."

She looked up at him with full trust and dependence. Yet she began to tremble, her mind questioning her Arabic fate.

Josh drew her quaking body close to him.

"We have to decide our lives for ourselves." Desperately, wildly, Josh glanced a few feet away at the limestone walls glowing in the shadows. "I read that in the rear wall behind the mausoleum in the hall," he murmured, "there is an opening." Separating from Haja, he crossed to the blocks of limestone and moved his hands along the bottom of a hanging tapestry to its far edge. He felt a raised bulge. Quickly, he pushed up the fringe and saw, in the dim light, a bolted lock. He reached into his boot, pulled out an Army knife, and pried the lock open. Cut into the limestone he found a door and swung it open. Using his Army flashlight, he saw the dark walls of a tunnel.

"Haja...let's leave," Josh whispered. "Let's go! Come on! Get the chair. It will keep everybody away from us!"

"What about your strength?"

"What about yours?" Josh smiled. "You said lovers have extra strength."

Haja ran for the chair. Unexpectedly, it felt heavy.

Awkwardly, she pushed it toward Josh. Impatiently, he put two spare bottles of oxygen in its seat, along with a few supplies and scooped up several flashlights.

They entered the tunnel and Josh closed the door tightly behind him.

The tapestry swung back in place.

⤛

In the noon sunshine on the outer road up to the Tomb of the Patriarchs...

A PA blue police car leading the military convoy braked to a swift halt. Emerging from the still rolling BMW, General Ali Salmah uttered a series of Arab oaths at waiting guards. A formidable, medal-chested figure in a heavy blue uniform, he cursed them for allowing foreign infidels to penetrate the Patriarchs' shrine. Seconds later, smoothing his dark hair and forcing a smile on his wide, large-nosed face, he opened the rear sedan door and helped Dr. Ramzy to stand on his canes. In his long white medical coat, the doctor straightened his pained body. His eyes widened at the sight of navy-blue uni-formed police leaping out of cars and trucks. Behind them, he glimpsed two Abrams halftracks with mounted machine guns, and two T-134 cannon tanks approaching both sides of the mosque's broad entranceway.

General Salmah helped Dr. Ramzy up the wide slate steps, followed by the Rose of Sharon group, and on their flanks, in bul-letproof vests, the IDF's twenty-soldier helicopter task force on one side and on the other a platoon of helmeted PA military men armed with riot shields, grenade launchers, and AK-47's.

"Joshua can be hurt!" Estee Isaacson called in English. She pushed away some of the weapons soldiers held in their hands. "Stop. This is awful!"

Imam Ishmael urged PA soldiers forward with a raised fist. "Force the doors! Save my daughter!"

"You cannot shoot!" Nurse Tarcai shrieked in her Irish Hebrew. "You cannot shoot patients of hospital!"

"We have to talk to them—no shooting!" Captain Cohen spoke in Arabic to General Salmah.

"All this force is not necessary. This is excessive!" Dan Isaacson pleaded in both languages.

"Excessive force—" General Salmah answered the Isaacsons in English without slowing his footsteps, "is a tactic of your American general Colin Powell. Advance with overwhelming force. Shock and awe. It makes the enemy surrender."

"Those inside are not enemies. They're under medical care." Dr. Ramzy spoke Arabic compellingly, repeating it in English.

"The people inside broke into our sacred tomb!" The General's meaty hands signaled his soldiers forward.

～

Behind the ornate, bolted doors of the mosque...

Frenzied searches throughout the large hall had not turned up Josh, Haja, or her wheelchair. Noor was frantic with worry. Outside now, sounds of rumbling tanks, loud voices, and approaching heavy footsteps grew louder. Brother Byron waved his observers to positions near the entrance, looked skyward, and inhaled a determined breath. He switched his microphone on. "Halt!" He shouted in Arabic, and repeated in Hebrew. "Stop!"

∿

On the mosque's entranceway broad steps...

"Stop!" The third command, in English, resounded in the open air from two Cedars of Lebanon trees.

It was followed by these English words: "Twenty official witnessess—priests, nuns, and civilians stand together in the Tomb of the Patriarchs. Do not enter! They will report misconduct by either PA or IDF forces to their churches in Europe, the Americas, and Asia. This conversation is being recorded in universal English. The world will hear every word!"

"An authorized police and military force," General Salmah promptly shouted in English at the loudspeakers, "is massed against whoever you are. Open the doors of the mosque!"

"Do not fire weapons at us!" The gravel voice that came from the speakers was clipped and clear.

"You have broken Hebron's civil and religious law," General Salmah called back. "All of you will be arrested. Now!"

"Listen to us." The loudspeakers sounded.

"First, open the doors!"

"Today, at ten o'clock this morning in Tel Aviv," the sound system rang out, "a wheelchair filled with explosives was set to blow up the Rose of Sharon Hospital—its patients, doctors, and personnel. That wheelchair is with us in the tomb. Sudden force can blow up you and us in the same second."

General Salmah slowed. One hand shot into the air. Movements of the military police and the civilians abruptly froze.

"The superintendent in charge of the Sharon Maintenance Department will speak now." The loudspeaker system continued.

"Last night, I packed fuel oil and nitrate into the tires and tubes of this wheelchair." The new, nervous speaker voice sounded determined. "Enough to turn the entire five-story hospital and buildings around it into a fireball. I did this at the request of Imam Ishmael bin Kanaan. If he is there with you, ask him if it is not true."

Gasps arose among the crowd. People shrank back in horror from the imam as four IDF soldiers moved in and separated him from Al-Jabbar and a shocked, frightened Carol Ann Tarcai. Their guns ringed him in a circle.

"Traitor to your people!" Ishmael's Arabic rasped into the air. He raised his fist. "You have betrayed Allah!"

"It is you who have betrayed Allah!" Rashid's English words blared from the loudspeakers. "In the past I followed you! Through the one God and his prophet Muhammad, I follow Allah directly now. He said, 'Follow up a bad deed with a good one and the good deed will wipe the bad out.' You have kidnapped three of my daughters. In Muhammad's name," Rashid's voice broke down, "in Allah's name, release them!"

"General, sir—" Al-Jabbar stepped forward, his voice shaking with fear. "Last night, our wheelchair disappeared. I think Rashid has it. It is very dangerous."

"Does he speak the truth?" General Salmah turned to the imam.

Ishmael stared back, narrow eyes defiant, lips pressed together.

"I recognize your voice," Rafael Ramzy pointed one of his canes at the tomb doors. "You are our engineer, Rashid. This is Dr. Ramzy, Sharon's Chief of Surgery. Why did you come to the Tomb of the Patriarchs?"

"Your questions, sir," came Rashid's reply, "the brother will answer."

"What brother?" Dr. Ramzy asked.

"I am Brother Byron." The composed, gravelly voice returned to the loudspeakers. "I'm a Franciscan friar."

"Why have you interfered?" General Salmah broke in.

"We follow St. Francis the Catholic, and Jesus the Jew. We live by the principle, 'The Lord gave me brothers.'"

"Temporary international observers, are you all?" General Salmah shouted, streams of perspiration from the noon sun running inside his heavy uniform. "You *Tippies* are forbidden to interfere in police incidents. I am the Palestine Police Commander for the West Bank, General Salmah. I command you to open this mosque!"

"General," Captain Cohen warned. "The mosque is also a sacred temple."

"I will say why the Tomb of the Patriarchs is sacred." Brother Byron's voice boomed smoothly and clearly. "First I must say why we left from the hospital last night. It was because two Sharon patients badly injured in this war, a Muslim and a Jew, fell in love. I married them Tuesday midnight. Yesterday, the father of the Jew, Doctor Isaacson, secured airplane passage to kidnap his son to America to break the marriage. The father of the Muslim, Imam Ishmael bin Kanaan, commanded his daughter to be a suicide bomber this morning, blow up herself, her husband of two days, and hundreds more of us. I brought them both here."

"Why here?" Dr. Ramzy demanded.

"Francis of Assisi, the holy founder of my order, had a vision in the thirteenth century," Brother Byron spoke calmly, "to rebuild God's church on earth. While I was in silent prayer, hours after I witnessed the marriage of Lieutenant Joshua Isaacson and Haja bin Kanaan, I had a similar vision. During my prayer, a voice seemed to say, 'In order to repair the church on earth, bring these newlyweds back to Abraham, the founding father of all children of the Middle East.' Therefore, we came to the Tomb of the Patriarchs."

"How can your visit restore the church on earth?" Dr. Ramzy asked.

General Salmah flung up his arm, Micro-Uzi pistol in hand. Rifle fire rent the sultry air. In the trees beside the mosque entrance, the Bose speakers abruptly disintegrated. Two PA soldiers lowered their rifles. The military police platoon ran with their commander up the final broad steps to the entrance. With his pistol, General Salmah shot off the mosque's ornate door handles. A group of PA's hammered AK-47 butts against the mosque doors. In less than a minute, the doors flew open.

PA and IDF soldiers with raised rifles rushed inside. Shouts and screams in different languages filled the hall. Friars, nuns, and civilians were wrestled to the ground. Noor was taken captive. Rashid and Brother Byron had their arms savagely pinned behind their backs.

"Haja? Haja?" Ishmael searched through the hall. "Haja…"

General Salmah fired his pistol and smashed the recording machine.

"That won't do any good," Brother Byron shouted in English. "There's another machine recording the words!"

"Where is it?" General Salmah aimed his gun.

"I won't tell you!"

"Joshua?" Estee Isaacson shouted, "Joshua? Joshua—"

Dan Isaacson grabbed Noor by her coat. "Where is my son?"

"This whole affair is a fake, huh?" General Salmah turned on Brother Byron. "There is no chair!"

"They have taken it!" Noor struggled to get free. "Haja and the lieutenant have gone with the chair!"

"That hospital wheelchair, he said—" Dan Isaacson pointed at Rashid, "is filled with explosives. They can be killed!"

Dr. Ramzy waved his canes sadly, his mind on his father. "Then all of us can be killed now."

❦

Below the Tomb of the Patriarchs, in the dark, rock-strewn tunnel…

Slowly, Josh and Haja pushed their weighted wheelchair yard by yard over stones and between boulders. Josh used a flashlight intermittently to conserve the battery. In the biting cold air, both of them labored for breath.

Haja began coughing repeatedly. Josh quickly unstrapped his oxygen concentrator and passed the nosepiece to her. She managed a few inhalations, and he took some gulps, also. He took a blanket from around the supplies on the chair and covered her shivering body.

After a few more steps, Haja dropped her hands from the chair and doubled over against the stony wall, gasping "The chair is too heavy for us."

"As long as we keep it with us, they won't come close. We've only gone a short way."

"We have no more strength."

Josh played his light onto the rock faces of the tunnel. "The walls are icy! That means somewhere there's an opening! That means somewhere—escape. Haja, we'll get free."

"Free to be captured? Torn away from each other?" Haja slipped to the gravel floor. "Free to be murdered in honor killings?" Acknowledging an ancestral fate, she dropped her head between her knees.

Josh inched down the wall and drew her in to share the warmth of his body. In the inky blackness, he heard a faint humming from Haja's throat. Then he recognized her weak voice singing the English words she sang at Sharon when they first met.

"Hand me the flute, and hum, for escape is the best remedy,
For people are nothing but lines, written in water…"

Haja raised her pencil flashlight and played it on Josh's exhausted, pale face. She ran a hand through the waves of his sandy hair. "When I was filled with despair," she whispered, "you gave me hope. When I was filled with hate, you gave me love." Her gaze rested on his eyes that always brought to her mind the sun on the Mediterranean Sea. "Allah knows with all our hearts we love each other. But love is no match against our enemies. Our parents are our enemies. Our peoples are our enemies. Go, sweet husband, while you have a chance. Be free without me." She remembered Carol Ann's words and repeated them. 'Such is my love, to thee I so belong … that for thy right, myself will bear all wrong.'"

Josh rose to his feet. He flashed the light about them and saw nothing but grim black walls. He sucked in a deep breath. His eyes filled with determination, he reached down for Haja's limp shoulders and struggled upwards, steadying them both on their feet. He put one hand around her and grabbed onto the chair with the other, slowly pushing forward among the boulders.

The tunnel turned sharply. The black air turned shadowy grey. Josh tapped Haja until her eyes opened. Through the rough surface above their heads, they clearly heard Brother Byron's voice.

~✕

Inside the crowded, carpeted Tomb of the Patriarchs mosque floor…

"Why is this Tomb of the Patriarchs sacred to each person who hears my voice, and to all religions?" From a slightly raised platform, Brother Byron's words reached throughout the tomb. "Because buried here is the first prophet who believed there was one God. In the Qur'an is this prophet not called Ibrahim? In the Bible is he not called Abraham? Who were the first two sons of this prophet? They were Ishmael, through his Arab mother, Hagar, and Isaac, through his Jewish mother, Sarah. So Ishmael and Isaac were brothers! Standing here among us right now are two descendant sons of these brothers—Ishmael bin Kanaan and Daniel Isaac-son!"

Friars and nuns in the hall translated Byron's words into Hebrew and Arabic. Shocked murmurs broke angrily from among the listeners.

Brother Byron stretched his robed arm toward Ishmael. "This man's daughter bears the given name of Hagar. She married Joshua, this man's son…" Byron pointed at Isaacson. "Chase their children. Capture them. Kill them! Whom do you capture or kill but the children of your own family, the descendants of the prophet some of you honor as Abraham, and some as Ibrahim!"

Byron barely waited for his words to be translated. "From the descendants of Ibrahim's son Ishmael, descended Muhammad, prophet to millions of persons. From the descendants of Abraham's son Isaac, descended Moses, prophet to millions of persons. From Moses, descended Jesus the Christ, prophet to more millions. All descended from one family! Rather than use this tomb to make war on Haja and Joshua, can we not use this hall as a place for Muslims, Jews, and Christians to see they are our children?"

～✺

On the tunnel floor, huddled for warmth together…

In the gloomy darkness Josh and Haja listened with enthralled attention. They waited to hear the reactions from their parents and their police persecutors. But the next voice from the hall above them was in English, tinged with heavy Hebrew inflections.

"I can add to this family story. I am Dr. Levinson, the director of Sharon's blood bank." The youthful voice pulsated from side to side of the tunnel. "Early yesterday morning at the hospital, Isaacson's son stood in urgent need of a blood transfusion. Under our microscope we discovered that Ishmael's blood was a safer match than the blood of both Isaacson and his wife!"

Haja and Josh clasped hands and exchanged glances in the murky darkness.

"So the son recovered due to the injection of blood from Ishmael. Early this morning at the hospital, Isaacson informed us of a probable cure he had uncovered for the poison in the lungs of Ishmael's daughter, Haja. As soon as we locate her we can begin her recovery!"

Electrified, Haja and Josh struggled to their feet. "Haja! Hagar!" Tears sprang to Josh's eyes. "You're going to live!"

"So will you! Joshua, my husband!" Haja hugged him to her. "I thought my lips would never touch you. Soon we can kiss!"

"My father did help you!"

"My father did help you!"

They laughed and cried; and cried, and jumped for joy. Above their heads, a deep voice began to speak. "That's the number one doctor at the hospital," Haja said. "Listen—"

⟞⟝

From a low stand at a mosque side wall, held securely by Nurse Noor...

"Friends or enemies, all of you here with me," Dr. Ramzy

said, slowly forcing his crippled body upright, "parents, military, medical, and religious persons, at any moment, this sacred building that holds four thousand years of our history, can be blown to the skies, with us included. Therefore, my words must be to the point."

Listening to his English words turned into Hebrew and Arabic, the doctor raised his voice. "Brother Byron said billions of Muslims, Jews and Christians—indeed, all who believe in one God—belong to one family. His words described the religious history of everyone in this sacred place of worship. In simple words, our family.

"At Rose of Sharon, we were shown the medical history of our family. It was shown that whether you use the name Ibrahim or Abraham, his sons were of one blood. They were brothers! But our family has another history. A history of memory."

Rafael's voice deepened. "Through centuries of recorded time, in peace and in war, our family lived side by side. Into our memory, we built a record of tolerance for each other, of dependence and affection for each other. We also built a record of fears and falsehoods, feelings of inferiority and superiority, and a lust to hate and kill each other.

"I know. I was born in Egypt. My ancestors' last name was Ramses. My father told me I am descended from King Ramses, the pharaoh of Egypt, a sworn enemy of the Jews. I am a Coptic Christian, a strong defendant of the Christian faith!"

The doctor looked at Noor. With her assistance, he struggled out of his hospital coat, and General Salmah, Captain Cohen, and some others exchanged bewildered glances.

With agonizing struggle and effort, Rafael thrust his head almost to his full six-foot-four-height. "I removed my coat," he declared. "It was very difficult for me. Not only because of my physical problems, but because as a member of the Christian faith, it was my heavy coat of memory."

Rafael extended his arms. "When I stretch out my arm to Ishmael, a Muslim with his heavy coat of memory, and my other arm to Isaacson, a Jew with his heavy coat of memory, will they keep them on? Or will they take them off… join my hands in our one family?"

Everyone in the mosque seemed to hold their breath.

Dr. Ramzy remained with his arms painfully outstretched. Noor steadied him.

A loud, scraping noise came from the rear of the building. Dr. Ramzy and the crowd turned as one toward the far wall of the mosque as the hanging tapestry tipped out of place, Josh and Haja emerged from behind it.

"We were in the tunnel. We heard what you said," Josh called out. "We want to join our family." They moved purposely toward the front of the mosque, their hands in front of them guiding the wheelchair.

Ishmael bolted across the mosque floor. In less then ten long strides he wrenched the chair out of their hands and slanted it sidewise.

"The chair is a bomb!" Al-Jabbar shouted. "It's a live bomb!"

"No! I cut the wires!" Rashid yelled.

PA police and IDF soldiers began raising weapons.

Ishmael rushed the wheelchair across the carpets toward the iron gate that ringed Isaac's Tomb.

"I put them back! I joined them back up! It's a bomb!" Al-Jabbar howled.

"Don't shoot!" Haja begged. "Abouya, stop!"

"Give us a chance to live!" Josh screamed.

The IDF soldiers with their rifles trained on Ishmael were too paralyzed with fear to fire.

Ishmael aimed the chair's front left wheel directly at the gate's corner metal post.

Dan Isaacson dashed to the tomb, flinging himself in front of the gate. "We are brothers!" he shouted. He blocked the gate with his body. "Ishmael, here is my hand!"

"You steal my land with the other one!" Ishmael yelled

Isaacson threw out both arms. "Take both my hands!"

Ishmael swerved the chair toward a corner gatepost further away.

"What do you want?" Isaacson shouted, running after him, flinging himself against a portion of the iron railing. "What do you want from me, brother?"

Ishmael raised his eyes from the chair. He sucked air into his chest. His head tilted ever so oddly at Isaacson for an eternity of seconds. He stared into the Jew's eyes. *What do you want from me, brother?* He heard an answer forming in his brain welling from a memory as old as his Canaanite forefathers.

"Treat me … " his voice was hoarse, "like you treat yourself."

The unexpected reply slipped past Isaacson's defenses, exploding into his mind. *Treat me like you treat yourself.* Sudden tears welled up and clouded his vision as an unguarded sense of truth struck in his solar plexus and deep in his memory bank.

"Daniel," Estee was at his side, extending the scarf he had given her, "In *Song of Songs*, in the Old Testament, "the desert rose of Sharon whom King Solomon loved—was an Arab, a *Shulamite* queen."

"In Islam—" Ishmael cried out, "She was Bilqis. The queen of my ancestors!"

Dan Isaacson looked at his wife. Then his eyes found Haja and his son, their hands tightly clasped.

Carol Ann Tarcai stepped forward and touched Ishmael's robe. "We are one family!"

A breath escaped Dan, of truth, anguish, righteousness, and guilt.

Ishmael's gaunt body swelled upwards. "Treat me like you treat yourself," he repeated, simply.

"I will." The words escaped Dan. "I promise I will!"

But then he took a new breath. He folded his arms across his stout chest. "When I invite you into my home. When you sit at my table," he looked squarely at Ishmael. "When you eat the food my wife prepares—what will prevent you from drawing a knife concealed in your robe and killing my family?"

Ishmael's eyes glowed with his truth of centuries. "Repeat after me. Allahu Akbar."

Dan Isaacson looked into Ishmael's eyes. He searched for an answer he was not sure he could find.

Josh stepped forward. He responded both for his father and himself. "Allahu Akbar," he declared.

Dan Isaacson glared at his son, and immediately focused on Ishmael. "Repeat after me. Baruch HaShem!"

Ishmael's lips clamped together.

Haja quickly moved up to her father's side. Putting a firm hand on his arm, she spoke for them both. "Baruch HaShem!"

Josh and Haja warily steered the wheelchair away from the gate.

Captain Cohen looked at General Salmah. Impulsively, both uniformed men clasped each other's hands. Noor flung herself proudly at Brother Byron. Estee Isaacson threw her arms about Josh. Rashid doubled over the wheelchair and disarmed its undercarriage. The mosque exploded in pent-up joy.

Admirers mobbed Doctor Ramzy. Haja embraced her father, crying to him in English. "Joshua came to our house, Abouya. Our walls tumbled down!"

Carol Ann Tarcai began doing a high stepping riverdance, singing *"Joshua fought the battle of Jericho, Jericho, Jericho. Joshua fought the battle of Jericho…"* She seized Ishmael by one hand and took Dan Isaacson's arm with her other and coaxed both men to move their feet and sway from side to side. Noor took Carol Ann into a new circle with Haja and Noor. The nuns joined them. The soldiers laid their guns down. Soon, a circle of men and a circle of women moved around the floor. Nuns, friars, soldiers, doctors, nurses and hospital employees danced and chanted in different customs and languages.

The circles parted and brought Josh and Haja into the center and reformed around them, singing, *"Joshua fought the bat-*

tle of Jericho, Jericho, Jericho! Joshua fought the battle of Jericho. And the walls came tumbling down!"

Outside of the Tomb of the Patriarchs, rose of Sharon blossoms bloomed in the full desert sunlight.

Inside the mosque, the pearl wheelchair stood abandoned and ignored.

Los Angeles, Ca.,
March, 2010

afterword

The kernel of *Courage to Love* came via two *New York Times* news items that startled me; one, that both Jewish and Palestinian war wounded were treated in the same municipal hospital in Israel; two, that a few families of dying Arab soldiers willed the vital physical parts of their children to Jews in need of them, and vice versa.

Further, the seeds of this novel came from the realization that two of my friends are first-named Mohamad and Jacob. More to the point, over the past ten years I learned that their emotions for me ran as deep as mine for them. In other words, each one of them became my brother. One night, Mo had a toothache and I drove him to an after-hours drugstore. He, an academic scholar, painstakingly edits my writings to this day. Jacob plays ball with me even though he's many years younger and could find stiffer competition. No matter what we say to each other and to each other's wives, we are courteous and respectful, sensing our bonds.

My forty-year second marriage has also played a part in the creation of this love story. My wife's parents were Canadian citizens born in Lebanon who immigrated to the USA, and my parents were Americans from Austria and Russia; yet when the two of us met, both single after eight years, we were individuals, free enough to feel instantly that we were kindred spirits who could love and respect each other. An hour after we met, this petite, accomplished future wife told a friend on the phone that she had just met the man she would marry. I, on the other hand, did not call her for a week, instinctively prepping myself to meet the demands of a woman in that fullest meaning—a blend of strength, vulnerability, compassion, loyalty, intuition and wisdom.

"For all who dare to love," is the subtitle of *Courage to Love*. Those words were not idle ones for I have discovered that love is a purifying journey not only to one's heights but also a descent to one's torturous depths.

For example, here are published poems written during the midst of that discovery:

I Made a Little List

I made a little list! I made a little list!
Of things I must get rid of

To make myself honest! To make myself honest!
Desire, in all appearances, power, money, fame,
Fancy cars, Cuban cigars, pretty faces,
posh vacation places—
These things have made my list!

They never will be missed!
Fear, in all disguises,
Fear to learn, to grow, to change,
Hiding, lying, criticizing, blinding eyes to nature—
These things have made my list!

They never will be missed!
Love, in all selfish, avaricious tit for tat,
Love's forever, just you stay thin not fat,
Flatter me, agree with me, be my color, nationality—
These things have made my list!
They never will be missed!

Hate in all its finery,
Brutality and tyranny, mockery and snobbery,
Blasphemy and prophecy, jealousy and
self-pity and just plain grumpy me—
These things have made my list!

They never will be missed!
These things I must get rid of
To make myself honest! To make myself honest!

A few paragraphs earlier, I alluded to the fact that I have been
aware of those who left this plane of existence in wars. Here is
the expression of that feeling in poetry.

July 23, 1997

Today, worldwide newspapers,
Published a list of 2000 non-residents,
Whose bank accounts with the Swiss,
Have been dormant since World War II,
And are presumed to belong to Holocaust Jews,
And others who went to the ovens,
In and near Auschwitz.

First on the list was Joe, last was Karl,
In between were Albert, Jack, Jenny, Pearl,
Robert, George and Marie, Jeanne and Pierre, Natalie,
Names from 59 Countries: GBR ESP, CHN FRA
GER CZE, USA ITA...
What human heartbreak pours off this page,
What human tragedies we could have saved,
What needless tears went up to heaven,
From WW II 'till July 23, 1997

Do we really see,
These names, these countries,
Come down to how I treat you,
And how you treat me?

As a writer, I chose not to write fictional works for several
decades because I wanted to write more than stories with made-
up endings. I wanted what I did not possess—a meaningful
vision of the life we all live. As an observing child of the Great
Depression, one hundred wars, the Western, Asian and African
holocausts, the rise and fall of Communism, and the dizzying
growth of capitalism, nationalism, and the internet. I was full of
the world's woes, pleasures and desires. But I had not examined,
explored nor discovered my own self. My orders to myself were
to drop my ego, get out into the world: touch and taste, sense
and suffer, fail and triumph, fight and discover my own visions.
Those thoughts are in this poem:

The USA and Me

Rushing through life,
Childhood, teens, jobs, wives, kids,
We stub our toes, self-righteously,
Howling through the pain,
We set sail again,
So intent on success,
We can't see what's gonna happen to us.

We live life, forwardly,
Try to understand it, backwardly.

Inevitably, we rush toward Armageddon,
Personal, to me; to the USA, 9/11,
At the same time, unexpectedly,
We run into the unseen, mysterious
reality of love,
Slowly, love dissolves our terror, anger, fear,
Slowly, love purifies our humanity,
We stop rushing,
Forwards and backwards, compulsively,
We begin, to be.

glossary of arabic, hebrew & medical terms

Aatini Nay: Hand Me the Flute, a pop ballad sung by the distinguished Lebanese singer Fayrouz from a poem by the poet Khalil Gibran, in Arabic.

Abouya: Father, in Arabic.

Aleikhem shalom: And peace unto you, in Hebrew.

Allahu Akbar: God is great, in Arabic.

Al Mahmoudiya Mosque: historic Muslim house of worship overlooking Jaffa harbor.

Ana bihkysh Englesi: I don't speak English, in Arabic.

Ana bihkysh Hebrew: I don't speak Hebrew, in Arabic.

Ankylosing spondylitic: rare, progressive form of arthritis affecting the spine and large joints.

Awedak: I promise, in Arabic.

Baruch HaShem: Blessed be the Name, in Hebrew.

Bilqis: Arabic; a beloved wife of King Solomon. In Islamic tradition, the Queen referred to in Habeshan history, the Hebrew Bible, the New Testament, and the Qur'an as the woman who ruled an ancient kingdom of Sheba, which may have included Eritrea, Ethiopia and Yemen. She is described as alluringly beautiful, and black as the tents of Kedar, (usually made of black goats hair).

Chador: all-enveloping dark garment for women worn by some Muslims and Hindus.

Coptic: belonging to the Egyptian Monophysitic (belief in single nature of Jesus Christ as both human and divine) Christian Church.

Essenes: Second Century BC to first century AD brotherhood of holy men and women: credited with the maintenance of the Dead Sea scrolls and bringing forth people who changed the course of history, including St. Ann, Joseph and Mary, John the Baptist, Jesus, and John the Evangelist.

Fatihah: refers to the opening chapter of the Qur'an.

Gaza: largest city in Gaza Strip and the Palestinian Territories, founded in the 15th Century BCE: one of the oldest, and most densely populated areas on earth; approx. 1.3 million Palestinians and a sprinkle of Christians in a small area twice the size of Washington D.C. From a self governing Canaanite/ Hebrew trading center on the Egypt-Syrian caravan route, Gaza fell under the rule of multiple nations: ancient Egypt, the Philistines, Neo-Assyrians, Neo-Babylonians, Greece,

Rome, the Maccabees, the Arab Empire, Egypt, Turkey, the League of Nations, the Palestine Liberation Organization, and afterwards, through 2004, Israel. *In 2007, the Islamist group, Hamas, became the elected leadership of Gaza.*

Go Mbeannai Dia duit: May God bless you, in Gaelic.

Hagar: a wife of Ibrahim who was a prophet of God and an important prophet in Islam, as narrated in the Qur'an. Hagar and Ibrahim were the parents of Ishmael, the first-born son to Ibrahim.

Hijab: Headdress, scarf, veil; used by Muslim and non-Muslim women.

Hummus: garbanza bean paste, a favorite Middle East dish.

Imam: Religious leader, caller to the Muslim faith, Islamic scholar.

Insha' Allah: God willing, in Arabic.

Intifadas: Shaking off, rebellions, Palestinian uprisings against Israeli rule.

Israel Defense Forces: (IDF) Israel's ground, air, and naval forces: Israeli citizens, males and females, serve for two and three years.

Jabaliya: (Jabalia) Refugee camp in Gaza Strip of 175,000 persons crowded in 1.4 sq. km., administered by the Palestine Authority, characterized by alleys, concrete and cinderblock shelters.

Jallabiya: Long garment worn by Muslims.

Jihad: In Islam religious terms, the struggle/an effort in worshipping Allah; Islamic campaign against nonbelievers waged by Muslims in defense of the Islamic faith

Kaaba: the cuboidal (cube) building in Mecca, Saudi Arabia. Thousands of years old, it is toward this building that all Muslims around the world face during prayer.

Kaffiyeh: Headdress fastened by a band, worn by Arab men.

Kufi cap: Knitted skull cap worn throughout the ages, often times with religious significance. A purple kufi is a symbol of the highest spiritual order.

Laparoscopy packs: Large, absorbent gauze towels; short name, "laps."

Ma' assalama: Peace be with you, in Arabic.

Ma'at: Truth; ancient Egyptian goddess of order, physical and moral law.

Maraba, kayfa halak: Hello, how are you? In Arabic.

Mazel tov: In Hebrew, good luck.

Mitzvah: Good deed, act of kindness performed by or to a Jew.

Moriah Mountain: (now the Western Wall, Jerusalem) sacred site to Arabs as the area where Ibrahim offered his son Ishmael to Allah; also sacred to Jews as the site where Abraham offered up his son Isaac.

Mossad: The Institute for Intelligence and Special Operations for the state of Israel.

Mujahid: activity in the struggle for Islam.

Neharak saeed: Good day, in Arabic, spoken to a male.

Neharek saeed: Good day, in Arabic, addressed to a female.

OR: Operating room in The Rose of Sharon Municipal Hospital.

Palestine Authority Military Forces: (PA) The Palestine Authority has approximately 30,000-50,000 security and blue-uniformed military personnel.

Pnuemonitis: inflammation of the lungs.

Qur'an: The Koran is the central religious text of Islam written by the prophet Muhammad during his life at Mecca and Medina.

RDX: Explosive material

Salaam Aleikum: Peace be on you, in Arabic.

Shabbas: Saturday, Jewish holy day.

Shahada: the act of becoming a martyr while fighting for Islam, in Arabic.

Shaheda: Female Muslim martyr, in Arabic.

Shalom: Peace, a greeting or leave-taking among Jews, in Hebrew.

Situ: Mother, in Arabic.

Song of Songs: a short book of the Hebrew Bible—or Old Testament, containing only 117 verses written by the king (1 Kings 4:32); also known as the Song of Solomon. The main characters are King Solomon and the queen of Sheba, who is described, literally, as alluringly beautiful and black as the tents of Kedar, (usually made of black goats hair).

Tabboulleh: Seasoned Mediterranean salad made principally with cracked wheat, parsley, mint, lemon, green onions and tomatoes.

Tetkallamy arabi: "Do you speak Arabic?" In Arabic.

Tippies: Temporary international observers in a foreign land.

The Forty Hadiths: popular book collection of the sayings of Prophet Muhammad.

WBC: White blood count.

Ya Elahy: Oh my God. In Arabic

Yahweh: Name for God. In Hebrew.

Yarmulke: A skullcap worn by observant Jewish males.

Zain: All right

Thanks for reading this book.
To contact the author, please write Tate Publishers
or send an email to: courage2love@me.com

Please consider making gifts of this book to those for whom you care—relatives, friends, opinion makers, young people, organizations and public libraries. Thank you.

Add to what others have said and done at:
www.couragetolovetheblog.com

Courage to Love is now available as a spell-binding CD.

The narrator is award-winning writer-director Bill Birrell, director and co-writer of "Purple Heart," and founder of Sony Pictures Imageworks. BIrrell is currently preparing "The Point Man," an inspirational bio-pic about a veteran who walks across America on his hands.

The audio version can be purchased at
www.tatepublishing.com
and anywhere books are sold.